The Feeling House

The Feeling House

Saleh Addonia

Holland House

www.hhousebooks.com

Paperback ISBN: : 978-1-910688-78-6

Cover design by Ken Dawson
Painting by Anna Leader

Typeset by Polgarus Studio

Published in the UK

Holland House Books
Holland House
47 Greenham Road
Newbury, Berkshire RG14 7HY
United Kingdom

www.hhousebooks.com

For Fineas

Contents

SHE IS ANOTHER COUNTRY

1

After the authorities refused us asylum and the court of appeal dismissed our appeal, we went underground. The grounds of our applications were to seek Her. In our applications, we stated that in the country where we grew up she was nowhere to be found so we fled to fall in love with Her.

While we were in the detention centre awaiting deportation, we tried to kiss Her; she was our lawyer. She was the first of her kind with whom we came close, face-to-face alone in a room. She dropped our case and asked us to find another lawyer, but we didn't bother.

We escaped the detention centre and walked into the city. On our way, we passed a park and spotted Her lying on her back in the green grass, one leg draped over the other. She was wearing yellow underwear, a pair of sunglasses, and was reading a book. We stopped near Her. We stared at her legs in wonder, very seriously. But before we could examine the rest of her naked flesh, she noticed us. She stopped reading her book, lifted her glasses and shooed us off.

We arrived at a contractor's office – an address we

obtained at the detention centre. As if the manager had been waiting for us, he stood up and got out from behind his desk. He was a man in his late thirties, fat but well dressed. He looked each of us up and down.

'Are you allergic to dust?' the manager asked.

We looked at each other and said, 'No.'

'Do you want to work as street sweepers?' the manager asked.

'Yes!' we shouted.

'You've got the job,' the manager said and walked back to his desk. 'You have to work hard. And please remember, you are easily replaceable.'

We were based in the city centre. We each used a two-wheeled trolley bin, a shovel, and a brush set. In addition to our uniforms – bright red overalls and gloves - we wore high-visibility yellow vests in the summer or jackets in the winter with bright red capital letters on the back that said:

FOR A CLEANER PAVEMENT

We cleaned in all weather conditions because getting the sack was unthinkable. We worried about our foreman and feared the authorities, though our job eased the latter – we wore our uniforms from home to work and vice versa. We swept dirt off the pavements and kerbs with our brushes and shovelled it into our carts. We collected the rubbish from the public bins and took them to collection points. While working, we ignored men and children and observed only Her. And she was everywhere around us. Our eyes enjoyed their new-found freedom as if they were at a banquet; they roved everywhere to spot Her. We were captivated by the variations of her face and its shapes, the texture of her skin.

And almost on a daily basis, we would be halted by a sudden spasm with a glimpse of her bare legs or arms or shoulders or cleavage or her well-rounded breasts or bum or miniskirt or tight trousers. We'd always get so excited. We'd feel her image taking possession. As if possessed, we'd put our shovels and brushes into our bins, but then we'd remember we had a job to do. We would think it was love at first sight and we'd spend hours talking about it.

We tried to draw her attention to us; we offered her our uninterrupted gazes, we stopped and sometimes bowed for Her to pass while we were sweeping, smiled when we saw Her approaching and on occasions we whistled politely when we saw Her walking on the other side of the pavement or when her back was turned to us. And sometimes we stopped working and took up a particular pose, pretending to look elsewhere as she passed or came out of a shop or appeared from a corner, in the hope she'd notice us.

Whenever we met after work in our room, sitting on the floor or lying on our bunk beds, she was the subject of our conversation. We talked about her face, which we concentrated on while at work so to familiarise ourselves with it. Each one of us tried to remember it and then argued about her hair, nose, eyes and lips. Sometimes we'd look for similarities between the face we'd remembered and the black & white pictures that we'd brought with us from the country we grew up in, which were now hanging on the wall above our beds. Or sometimes we'd look at the cut-outs from porn magazines that we stuck on the remaining walls, or some pictures from the tabloids that we'd look at daily. And God knows how we yearned to look at her bare flesh, beyond the fabric that covered some of her skin.

In our beds, we'd hear each other masturbating every

night; our dreams were the same.

One day while we were pushing our carts into the park for our lunch break we saw Her; her head was lying on his lap; he was sitting on a bench. Her eyes were closed; she seemed to be at peace, and he was staring down at her face in silence. We stood nearby and gazed at them without the man taking any notice of us. We left our carts somewhere in the park and sat on a bench to eat our lunch. Half an hour later, we looked at the couple again. The man's head was still in exactly the same position, looking down at Her and her eyes were still closed. We were astonished. We couldn't understand how the man would stare down at her face for that long without moving his head an inch. We thought we might have seen love at work.

'How would it feel if we were in love?' we asked each other.

'Perhaps, like him,' we answered.

In our room, we talked about what we would do if we fell in love with Her. We asked each other where we would take Her. We looked at the bunk beds and underneath the lower beds: shoes, food bags and luggage, old tabloid papers, porn magazines and ashtrays. Then we looked at the walls above the upper beds: there our clothes, including our uniforms, were hanging up alongside porn magazine cut-outs. We sat on Surag's bed and opened the shutters. Through the window, we looked at the tree in the garden, daydreaming. We dreamt of building a small cabin for Her. And we dreamt of Her lying next to us inside that cabin one morning. We'd wait for Her to wake up, and in the afternoon we'd sit under the tree with her head on our lap and we'd stare at her face for hours, like the man in the park.

We looked at each other. We smiled until we could see each other's teeth. But all of a sudden, we shouted, 'Aaaaaaaaargh!'

We went back to our beds, each of us sitting and looking at the one opposite, and we began to cry.

We saw Her thousands of times but she never once smiled, never returned our gaze nor took any notice, apart from those passing glimpses that weren't even directed at us but which were necessary to navigate her way. This was in stark contrast to our thoughts prior to arriving in the country. We thought she'd welcome us. We thought it was simple: love.

Over time, we stopped looking at Her in the streets. We threw away all the pictures of Her on our walls and stopped buying the tabloids. We stopped talking about love and romance. And when we played cards on the floor between our bunk beds, filling the tiny space with our bodies, we tried not to think about Her or imagine Her; we were tired of imagining. Yet we would see her limbs whenever we saw each other's limbs, our naked hands, legs, chests. Then we'd be afraid and we'd try to cover our faces with our hands. And when we were bored or tired of playing we retired to our beds. Our silence was only interrupted, from time to time, by a cough here or a limb movement there, a leg, hand, or head dangling over the bed. The only time we laughed was in the early mornings when one of us would wake up earlier than the others and hide Sami's hearing aid which he wore on his left ear. Sami would wake up and look for his hearing aid with increasing panic, before breaking into fits and shouts, and we'd spend 10 - 20 minutes looking for it with him.

Then came New Year's Eve. We were in the city's main square when the clocks struck midnight, and fireworks exploded and lit up the dark sky. Everyone around us jumped up and down, shouting, 'Happy New Year!' They kissed and hugged each other and danced. We looked on in silence, then followed the crowd and began shouting, 'Happy New Year!' and hugged one another. Then we saw Her in front of us.

'Happy New Year!' she said.

'Happy New Year,' we said.

She kissed one of us on the mouth, we stared with our eyes wide at each other, and soon we all hurried to kiss Her. When we kissed Her, we felt her tongue moving inside our mouths, so we moved ours too. It felt so good when the tongues licked each other. Her lips were so warm despite the weather being so cold, and from her lips we tasted alcohol for the first time in our lives. We went on saying *Happy New Year* followed by kisses on the lips till the early hours.

We and many other street sweepers were cleaning the square on New Year's Day, early in the morning; we didn't sleep. All our thoughts were on the lips we kissed the night before. We kept counting them but we never agreed in the final number; sometimes it was 30 lips or 35, sometimes 39, 45 or 50; we had never felt this kind of joy and happiness in our lives before. We felt our journey wasn't wasted after all.

Later in the night, we discussed the reason for our migration: Her love. We were ecstatic, then got confused, then angry and rebellious. We were lost for days. But we never stopped thinking of the number of lips we'd kissed and the urge to kiss more new lips.

'The question,' we said, 'is to love or to fuck?'

We couldn't understand our question because, if we were honest, we knew neither fuck nor love. But we knew the kisses of all those lips on New Year's Eve. We smiled at each other. That night we said, then shouted, 'to fuck!'

The night was all but unknown to us. Apart from the night of New Year's Eve, our nocturnal outings were rare. That was due mostly to our constant fear of the authorities, and partly also because we were physically tired: we worked 6 days a week, 12 hours a day – sometimes extra shifts on Sundays.

One evening, Ahmed cut our hair. When it was his turn, Hagus cut Ahmed's hair, but he left some patches on the top of Ahmed's head. Then Negash tried to fix it, but he made it worse and made a bald spot on Ahmed's crown. In the end, Negash clean shaved him with a razor. Ahmed was furious and kept shouting at Negash. We calmed him down and convinced him that he looked good in a blue wool hat. We shaved and had showers, put on our new trousers, and looked at one another's naked torsos, all envying Surag because he was the tallest and had the best toned body of us all. We then put on our shirts and our new shiny black leather shoes, moisturized our faces and sprayed ourselves with cologne. We thought we looked good and wished we could have gone out like this instead of covering our clothes with our uniform overalls and shiny vests. If wearing our uniforms made us invisible to the authorities during the day, we thought, then perhaps the same would apply at night. Of course we were worried she may not like us in our uniforms, but we hoped she'd like our faces and our scent. We weren't that bad looking; we could even say we were handsome. And we were nice and thoughtful people, we'd treat Her like a lady. Anyway, we'd take off our uniforms if we were to meet Her in a secluded space or if she invited us to her home.

We went to a bar far away from the city centre and far away from where we lived.

We stood at the bar area and looked around; the bar was half full. People were in groups, mostly of threes or more. Many of them were staring at us, or perhaps everyone was.

We felt uneasy about their stares. We tried not look at them; instead we turned around and looked at the bar. We didn't know what to order. We just kept looking at the beer taps and the bottles of whiskeys, vodkas and wines.

We saw Her walking towards us and made room for Her. She stood among us, put both hands on the bar counter. Her fingernails were painted dark red except her index and ring fingers, which were painted dark brown. She ordered half a pint of lager. She had a strong smell and her smell was so good. We stared at Her. She was really beautiful. Our dreams have come true, we thought. Then she smiled at us. And because of that little smile, we bent our heads away from Her and looked at each other. There were little tears in our eyes but they didn't come down and if they had they would have been tears of joy. For a minute or two we fought a private battle with our nerves, then said, 'Hello.'

'Hello,' she answered; her voice was friendly and sweet. We saw her teeth, fine white teeth.

We smiled and tried to think of something else to say; we wanted to talk to Her, communicate even a fraction of our feelings. But then she turned around, and a middle-aged man entered the bar and walked towards Her.

The man kissed Her passionately.

'I was waiting for you so impatiently,' she said.

'Really?' the man said.

'Yes, yes!' she said.

'I was in a horrible mood, too! Seeing you changed everything,' the man said.

'Oh, you make me so happy! How I wish I could be with you all the time,' she said.

'How sorry I am that I can't be,' the man said.

'You are sorry? Really?' she said.
'Really,' the man said.

She and the man took their drinks and sat at a table nearby.

We looked away, then into one another's eyes, and then ordered half pints of lager. The barmen seemed unwelcoming and one of them served us with cold eyes and an expressionless face.

Our first sips tasted so bitter; after we drank more we felt dizzy, but a bit more relaxed. We turned and looked around. We saw some people still throwing us those odd glances. But we didn't mind or perhaps even enjoyed it compared to our experience on the streets where nobody took notice of us.

We stared at Her. She looked at us briefly and then carried on talking to her partner. We then immersed ourselves in Her; our bodies were feeling sensations that made us stare at Her for more than half an hour. Our stares were uninterrupted, except for the people walking to and fro in front of us. While we stared, we'd take a sip or two from our glasses, and for the first time we felt the freedom of our gaze. We found ourselves taking in every detail of her face; the long black hair spread over her cheek, her fine long nose, her brown eyes, and her small lips painted in dark red. We followed every facial movement, and through them we imagined another reality for Her and us. Perhaps another life. And we wanted to plunge, right there, into this future and into her being. But as we were in the midst of all of this, she walked away with her partner without so much as glancing our way. We saw her complete profile and were awestruck by her long dirty-brown leather boots, short tight skirt and black fishnet stockings. As she vanished beyond the exit door, we looked at each other and felt a bit drunk; we had emptied our glasses.

Later on, we went to a club. There were two big bouncers standing outside the door; we smiled.

'What do you want?' one of the bouncers asked.

'To go in,' we said.

They looked us up and down one by one – we were standing in a line – and then looked at each other. One of them – we could see he was trying hard not to laugh – said, 'We don't need cleaners.'

'We aren't working now. We've just finished work and we want to dance,' we said.

'Do you have IDs?' one of the bouncers asked.

'What ID?' we asked.

'Passport or driving licence.'

'We don't drive but we have our passports at home. We live too far to—'

'Sorry. You need an ID to get in,' interrupted one of the bouncers.

'But we really want to dance tonight,' we said.

The bouncers stared at us unblinkingly, shook their heads, and said, 'No ID, no entry.'

'Aaaaaaaaaargh!' we shouted.

A third bouncer emerged from the club and stood with them. They all folded their arms across their chests, took a step back, and shouted, 'Go! Move! Move!'

As we walked away we heard the bouncers laughing.

At home, we were very angry and sad because we couldn't get into the club. We tried to forget the incident by watching porn and reading the tabloids. In one of the tabloids, we stumbled upon this headline:

HER MEASUREMENTS

It was an article about Her ideal size spread over four pages. There were many pictures of Her in Going Out Dresses and bikinis. Leafing through, we stopped at two pictures of an actress and remembered her face, the one we saw in the bar. We had no doubt that it was Her in the pictures. She was in a tight Going Out Dress and in a bikini. Her size was 36C–25-37 and her height was 5.4". We couldn't believe how beautiful she was in both real life and in the pictures. From then on, she became our new poster girl. We stuck her pictures on our walls and she was the one we'd think of whenever we'd masturbate.

The next day, still wearing our uniforms, we went to the same bar. The barmen seemed unhappy to see us again. One of them served us our half pints of lager without a word, with unfriendly eyes. We sat at the bar stools, but were very concerned by the barmen's attitude towards us. We talked to each other quietly about what we'd done the night before and whether we'd done anything wrong that could explain their behaviour, but we couldn't remember anything. We were occupying most of the bar stools. Some of us got off our seats.

We heard Her order two glasses of white wine and a glass of red; we turned to our right. She was wearing a black see-through long-sleeved shirt with her skin and black bra visible. And then we saw her fingers drumming on the counter. We wished those fingers had been drumming on our cheeks. She turned her eyes to us. They were enormous eyes. We smiled.

'Hello,' we said.

'Hello,' she said.

We smiled again. She looked at us one after another; she was beautiful with a fine long nose.

'Hello,' we said.

We smiled and waited for her to say something to us,

perhaps hoping she'd say, 'I was waiting for you impatiently.' But she stood and looked at us as if she was waiting for us to say something more. We said nothing, just kept on smiling. She was served and left, taking away her smile, her smell, her fingers. We thought how there was more to Her than her face, how it was also about talking to Her. The trouble for us was that we'd never talked to Her before. We'd talked to our lawyer but we'd only talked to Her about our cases. Our main problem was now how to get beyond hello. And what was in our heads beyond hello was fuck, nothing else but fuck.

The bar filled up. We had a few glasses of red and white wine. The music got louder and louder. People were dancing. Our eyes were dancing and darting trying to spot Her. We had many shots of whiskey. We got very drunk. We kept on opening and closing our eyes. We smiled a lot for no reason. We grimaced. We pulled each other's cheeks.

In the morning, we woke up with heavy hangovers. We were so sick that we thought we'd die. We ran to the bathroom one after another. We helped each other throw up into the toilet. Then we looked up at each other; tears were flowing. We helped each other into our beds, and we stayed there with horrible feelings and uncomfortable thoughts all day and all night. We thought about giving up.

Then one day we read a tabloid article entitled:

THE TEN BEST CHAT-UP LINES TO WOO HER

We spent the next few nights memorizing the lines.

Early on Friday night, we went to the same bar. When the two barmen saw us approaching they began to laugh and looked at each other. As we were about to order, they went into fits of laughter. We waited for them to stop. Then one of them said, 'What do you want?'

'We want to drink,' we said.

The barmen laughed again, and one of them said, 'Don't you remember last week?'

'Yes,' we said. 'We had a nice time here and we liked the music—'

The barmen burst into fits of laughter again, then one said, 'You tried to kiss Her... every woman in the bar... every...' and kept laughing . He turned towards the other barman, held him by the shoulders and tried to kiss him, but the other barman moved his face away in disgust. He then held his cheeks and tried to kiss him again, but again the other barman turned away. Embarrassed, we bowed our heads and left the bar with both barmen still roaring with laughter.

We bought beers from a shop and drank them on a street bench. Soon, we forgot the whole episode and talked about the chat-up lines.

Later, we were denied entry to every bar and club we approached. One evening as we made our way home, we passed a bar. Through the windows we saw a few people dancing and others drinking and talking. There was no one outside the door. We went in. The bar was a bit shabby; we didn't care. We ordered shots of whiskey and downed them in one go, one after another.

We saw Her dancing alone. She wasn't tall but well-proportioned, dark-haired, wearing black leggings with a tight black top. We began to dance in a line. Then slowly, we danced to the dance floor. And then danced around Her, held hands and circled Her; she was laughing and seemed to enjoy it, raising her arms and swinging her hips. We stopped dancing, moved close to her ear and shouted, 'Our dick just died. Would you mind if we buried it in your ass?'

She looked at us with her eyes and mouth wide open and then slapped us one after the other.

In the morning, when we woke up, we found Nigash's bed vacant with a handwritten letter near his pillow. We looked for him everywhere but couldn't find him. We read the letter aloud. It was addressed to his best friend in the country where we grew up:

Dearest Ali,

I was walking home to my girlfriend's flat after a few drinks on a night out with some friends. I passed a bar with a few people outside talking loudly. On the corner, I saw Her. She was standing alone against a wall. I stopped. She was pretty. She was crying silently, there were tears coming down her eyes. When she saw me, she smiled. I smiled. She smiled again and indicated to me with her index finger to come forward. I took a few steps forward. I said the first words that came to me, 'Where are you from?' with a low voice. She answered with one word but I didn't hear it. Despite this I moved closer and said, 'Are you?' 'Yes' she said. I moved closer still and said, 'Are you?' She nodded twice while looking at me with her big eyes. Her nose touched my nose and we both stared into each other's eyes. I took a step back. She smiled again and turned her head about 30-45 degrees to the right. I turned my head about 5-10 degrees in the opposite direction. She parted her beautiful big lips. I parted mine. She closed her eyes. I closed my eyes.

> *As I began to move my head slowly towards her, a woman's body came between us; she was my girlfriend and she was breathless. I forgot that I was near her flat...*

When we finished reading the letter we laughed out loud, but then we got sad. We hadn't written to our friends in the country we grew up in since we'd arrived in this country. Of course, we missed them and we knew they were waiting eagerly for our news; but we had no news to tell. We had made no progress in our mission. We simply couldn't tell them we had yet to find her love and that we'd had to change our plans and worse still that we were still wankers. But soon, we sat on our beds thinking about Nigash. It was unlike him, we told each other, to disappear like that. We were distressed but still put on our uniforms and left to go to work.

On our way there, we crossed a canal bridge. Not far from us we saw a police car and the fire brigade retrieving a body from the water. We walked slowly past them. We saw his dead grey face; he was wearing his normal clothes. We saw Nigash. We walked away quickly and cried at the next corner. We then told ourselves that Nigash's suicide shouldn't stop us from our mission. We have to carry on, we said to each other, no matter what, and went to work.

That evening as we were making our way home we stopped by a pub. We sat at the counter, looking down at our pints, with our eyes full of sorrow.

We heard Her say, 'Why are you so sad?'

We looked up; it was the barmaid. She was wearing a long-sleeved black shirt.

'We are looking for Her,' we replied, and looked down again at our pints.

'But she is everywhere,' she said. 'You've got to try.'

We looked up at Her. She had a long neck, she really had a long neck.

'I have a boyfriend,' she said.

'Who is your boyfriend?' we asked.

She pointed to the barman. The barman was serving someone at the far end of the counter.

'How long have you been with him?' we asked

'Eleven years,' she said.

'And how old are you?'

'Twenty five.'

'Eleven Years!' we shouted.

'Yes,' she said.

'Eleven years!' we shouted again.

'Yes!'

'How many times have you kissed him on the lips passionately in the last eleven years?' we asked.

'What?' she said.

'How many times have you fucked him in the last eleven years?' we asked.

All of a sudden her face was filled with wild anger. She said loudly, 'Out! Out! Get out!'

We walked out of the bar murmuring, 'Eleven years... eleven years... eleven years... and she is only twenty five!'

At home, with paper and pen we multiplied 365 by 11 and got 4015. 'Supposing her boyfriend fucked Her once every night,' we said, 'then he must have fucked Her 4015 times and he'll have one more tonight.'

4015 fucks, we murmured, 4015 fucks! And still counting! 'He had 4015 fucks!' we shouted. 'And we had none.'

We counted the number of wanks we'd had in our entire lives. We were in our mid-twenties and we'd been wanking since we were fourteen or fifteen. We wanked at least twice a day and sometimes even more. We multiplied our wanks – adding in our dead friend – and we hit tens of thousands.

'Tens of thousands of wanks!' we shouted. 'Tens of thousands!'

The next day, we were depressed. We couldn't stop thinking about Nigash or the man's 4015 fucks and our tens of thousands of wanks. But we cheered up a little when we remembered our conversation with Her in the bar. It was our first ever conversation with Her, we thought. But we felt down again when we reminded ourselves that she was the one who began talking to us. She was the one who asked us: *why are you so sad?* We concluded that we were decidedly unable to talk to Her or start a conversation. So we wrote a letter to Her. We also realized that to get into a good bar we had to go out early when there were fewer people and no bouncers at the doors.

One Saturday evening, we went to a bar.

She was wearing a large brown-framed pair of glasses and sitting alone reading a book. We handed Her the letter. It didn't take her long to read it, or perhaps she only read the first paragraph for she handed it back to us rather quickly. She put her book in her bag, gave us a freezing stare and walked away. We looked around and saw the barman looking at us. We walked to another table. We tried to hand Her the letter but she refused to take it. As we were begging Her politely, all of a sudden, the barman snatched the letter and began reading it. Halfway through, he began smiling. He finished reading the letter and said to us, lowering his voice, 'I will help you.'

The barman shouted out loud, 'I have an announcement

to make! I have an announcement!'

Everyone in the bar looked at the barman. We covered our faces with our hands, not knowing what to anticipate. The barman stood next to us, and read aloud,

'My dear You... In the country where we grew up, there was no You. They separated us from You everywhere, forbade all forms of communication between us and obliged You to cover yourself from head to toe so that we cannot remember if we have ever seen your face. Now, as You can see, we had no chance to meet or talk to You. We wanted to touch or kiss You, to love or make love to You—'

A drunk man shouted, 'Wankers!'

People were looking at us and we heard a few titters, but the barman said, 'Shhh,' and continued.

'You see, my dear You, the concept of love didn't exist in the country where we grew up and the authorities were applying all their might to prevent us from loving You. But once we reached a certain age, the pain of not loving You or being loved by You moved up from our hearts to our throats very slowly, and each time the pain reached our mouths we'd scream, 'Aaaaaaaaaargh!' We tried to resist. We were warned that the punishment for those caught trying was imprisonment or torture, or both, and for those caught in the act of love, it was the firing squad. We heard about the lucky few who fell in love and disappeared. But we too rebelled; we joined a secret organisation known as LRS: Love Rights Syndicates. LRS's main mission was to find You; someone willing to love and be loved. LRS would then put You in contact with one of its members who'd meet You at a secret underground location. Two years after joining, we were at the top of the waiting list, but then the organisation was discovered by the intelligence agencies and dismantled. Its leaders were caught, tortured and imprisoned indefinitely, and its members were sought out. It was then that we decided You were another country. Our journey was long and broken, treacherous and perilous. But that doesn't matter now because here we are to love You and seek a sanctuary in your bed. If it isn't possible to live in your bed, then please, let us visit it just once...'

The barman finished reading our letter. We looked around. We saw some people talking to each other as if they were debating our situation. We saw Her holding her partner's hand and giving us sympathetic stares as well as a few cold ones. We saw some men smiling or perhaps laughing, but that didn't bother us. We then saw Her walking towards us and past us with her eyes looking straight into ours; we smiled but she didn't; she just kept staring at us. We didn't understand the meaning of her gaze. As we were about to leave, the barman shouted, 'Come on boys, have a beer on the house.'

'Aaaaaaaaaargh!' we shouted in the barman's face, and walked away.

Early the next morning, we found Idris was missing. We looked for him and then, through the room's window, we saw a figure dangling from the garden tree by a rope. It was Idris. We hurried to the garden.

Idris was dead. We cut him loose and carried him to our room. We cried. We put Idris on his bed and covered him. Then we put on our uniforms and went to work.

In the dead of night, we dug a grave near the tree and buried Idris.

Days later, Ahmed was caught attempting to rape Her. And a few days after that, Surag decided to hand himself in to the authorities and take full advantage of their new amnesty programme for the voluntary return of failed asylum seekers to their countries of origin. But we refused to give up. We didn't want to accept that she was forever to remain an idea. Had we known our mission would have been so impossible, we wouldn't have ventured into this country. Perhaps, we thought, we should have chosen another country.

So we kept thinking until we saw Her staring at us. She was alone, standing at the bar. Her head was covered and she was wearing a smart green dress which stopped just above her knees. Her face was very beautiful.

She smiled at us, but we looked away.

A few moments later, we looked back at Her and she was still staring at us. She smiled at us and this time we forced ourselves to smile back. She smiled again. We smiled back. She picked up her drink and walked towards our table. We looked at her black high heels and then at her calves; they were long and well-toned. She pulled up a chair and sat among us. She looked at all of us in turn and then moved her head closer. We wanted to reach out our hands and touch her cheeks. She quietly said, 'Are you illegals?'

'What?' we said.

'Are you illegals?' she said, lowering her voice.

'What?' we said, and looked at one another as if to see whether we looked like illegals.

'You know what I mean,' she said. 'Are you illegals?'

We answered no, for we were afraid she'd be a plainclothes officer. She stared at us for a while, then smiled and whispered, 'Do you want a fuck?'

We stared in shock.

She stood up while looking at us. With our hearts pounding, we looked at Her. She picked up her drink, and as she was about to move away we shouted, 'Yes! Yes! We do.'

'Come with me,' she said, pointing at me.

I got up. I looked at Sami; he was crying.

I followed Her.

We entered Her room.

She closed the door and stood before it. I was about two or three metres away from Her and a few centimetres from her bed.

She took off her headscarf . She had no hair. Her head was smooth and bald. I looked at Her with my eyes wide open. She slowly began to pull her dress up; she wasn't wearing knickers. I saw her pubic hair. I went down on my knees.

She had a magnificent curved body.

She took off her bra, beckoned me over with her index finger, and said, 'Come. Come to Isabella.'

Her right breast was missing.

I didn't know how I opened my mouth but I didn't close it.

2

'... the trolley bin was positioned diagonally, directly facing the hole. Its handle was tied to the water pipe,' said the shopkeeper – a woman in her mid-thirties with hair tied back – and pointed to a black drainpipe at the back of the house.

'And where were you?' asked a local TV news reporter, a man in his early twenties.

'I was in the storage room upstairs. I was looking at him through that window,' the shopkeeper pointed up at a small window covered with black metal security bars on the first floor. 'He must have had started digging late at night.'

'What makes you think that?'

'I'm sure of it. I closed the shop at eight. I came back to

deliver more wood around 11. The wood was for a shed. They wanted—'

'They. Who are they?'

'They are young men. I am not sure how many they are. There are eight bunk beds in the room. We rent it to an agency—'

'Have you seen the others today?' interrupted the reporter.

'No,' said the shopkeeper. 'I don't know them. My husband only spoke to him and another one of his lot. They wanted to build a shed, here in the garden. They all live in the room above the shop. You access it by the staircase,' the shopkeeper pointed to an external rusty metal black staircase at the back of the house.

'What else did you see?' asked the reporter.

'He finished filling the trolley bin and took a rest. Then he went down the hole. Moments later, he came out and left through that door,' said the shopkeeper, pointing at a door leading to an alleyway. 'I came out to the garden. I inspected the rope that was attached to the pipe. It was very thick and tightly tied to the bin. The bottom of the bin sloped towards the hole, and was loosely tied to this tree.' The shopkeeper paused for a moment and rubbed her head. 'I looked at the hole,' she said. 'It was... I think it was 2 metres long and half a metre wide. I looked down the hole. There was a small chair inside. I stepped on the chair and went down into the hole. It was about... 2 metres high, I think... A bit higher than me.... Anyway, I went down on my knees and saw another hole dug on the side, level to the ground and the same length and perhaps the width as the first hole.' The shopkeeper held her head with one hand and took a deep breath. 'Anyway...inside the smaller hole I saw a couple of porn magazines and an unlit candle. I looked at the magazines. One of them was hard-core and the other soft-porn. I put back the magazines and hurried out of the hole. I was frightened. I was trying to understand what was going on. Then I heard him coming. I quickly ran back to the shop and went upstairs. I saw him inspecting the trolley bin. He then opened a new packet of cigarettes and took one out, but as he was about to light it he changed his mind and put it back. Then he took off all his clothes. He was naked. He looked up at his room and opened his mouth wide. I heard a scream. He turned and stood near the edge of the hole, looking at the sun and shading his eyes with his hand. He walked around shaking his head. He then held his lighter to the rope that was tied to the tree, and made sure it was burning before going down the hole. I then saw the chair tossed out of the hole. I looked at the burning rope. Nothing happened for some time. I was wondering what was going on inside the hole when, all of a sudden, the rope snapped. The trolley bin fell and dumped tonnes of soil into the hole...'

THE GIFT

"The sound! It's gone!" I shouted after waking from a coma in our round-shaped hut. But I could not hear myself. Only the tinny buzzing inside my head. I saw my family surrounding me, in tears. When I tried to get out of bed to enjoy the light of day, I felt dizzy and fell back, cradling my ringing ears. Family and friends came to the room and sat. They looked at me with pity then talked amongst themselves.

To avoid seeing people, I went out in the dark – in the moonless nights, and with father holding me with his right hand and the lantern with the other. Weeks later, my balance returned and my body strengthened. I got bored and ventured out. Adults and other children were greeting me with big smiles and thumbs ups as if I'd won something. Then their smiles wore out. They were replaced with waving and flailing hands, then with indifference and then with mocking.

One summer morning, I was sitting alone on the banks of the river, daydreaming; dreaming of being far away from this camp, alone and never to be found, when I saw a woman with striking tangled afro hair emerge from the bushes and into the river. She looked like an Eritrean People's Liberation Front fighter. The woman threw her bag on the riverbank and stripped naked.

I recognised her face. She was the singer I had seen the night before when the People's Front had their annual party. Many people sprayed paper money over her head and others placed their money on her forehead, and some women who didn't have money, threw their jewellery at her feet. Others danced near her, forming a circle and parading round slowly to the rhythm of her music. I didn't dance, nor hear what she sang.

The fighters would normally show up in the summer to entertain us. They sang, danced and performed plays to remind us about our duty to the revolution. They also took with them new recruits, some as young as 14, but father and mother weren't worried about me joining them, partly because I was deaf and partly because I was only 11. The woman walked and stood on the riverbed and splashed her body with water. She was tall and dark with muscular arms and legs, and two big breasts. The woman touched her belly gently and then swam in a leisurely way. She then turned over and floated on her back. Her belly protruding from the water like an ocean island.

It was then that I thought about *Red Flowers*. *The Red Flowers*, as mum told me, were the children born to female fighters who would be separated from their parents and raised in communal crèches away from the battlefields, so that their parents could keep fighting.

Later on, she got out of the river and while she was putting her trousers on, she noticed me. She looked at me and said something. I said nothing. She put the rest of her clothes on, walked and stood up in front of me. I got scared and shouted, 'I'm deaf!'

The woman smiled. She rubbed my head and then my cheek with her right hand in a friendly way. I saw the top part of her little finger was missing. She thought for a moment and wrote with her index finger on the sand: Can you read?

I nodded.

The woman took out a newspaper from her bag and handed it to me. I looked through the headlines but then I saw the woman's index finger pointing to a word: Fight. I looked up at the woman and ran away screaming, 'Nooooooo!'

I hid behind a steep slope and peeked up at her. The woman put both of her hands up and took a few steps backward. She left the newspaper where it was, waved goodbye with one hand and walked away.

After I made sure she had left, I went back and picked up the newspaper. I had never read a newspaper before. I looked at all the pictures first and then I began reading the paper. There were many new words to me; short and long. Sometimes, I didn't understand the sentences or in some cases, I could just about grasp the meaning. But that did not hinder me. I just read, page after page. I paid no attention to what was happening around me, it would be the same as yesterday. Children will arrive and play on the river bed, women will fill their water jugs or wash their children, men will come with their donkeys and fill their leather panniers with water, boys will jump into the river and swim and run away if they see a snake or two (no one will get drowned today, only once a year someone would drown here and it happened last Friday), travellers will cross the river by boat, birds will fly over. The light and heat will be the same with no clouds in sight. For a long time, I carried on reading and rereading the same paper until I persuaded my father, who was a tailor, to bring me a few newspapers from one of his visits to the city to replenish his fabrics.

I read and reread what my father brought me day and

night and ignored the world outside. Once my father noticed my love of this new world, he made an agreement with a newsagent in the city who kept for him each issue of a few newspapers. He would then pick them up whenever he was in the city. Within months, I had amassed hundreds of newspapers in our store hut and under my bed. I read and reread those newspapers every day from the moment I woke up until it was time to sleep. I read during family meals despite my father's objections. And when I got bored of the old papers, I read the papers that the shops where we bought our groceries would use as paper cones for goods such as rice, wheat, green coffee beans, salt, white sugar or spices. Sometimes, those papers were in a foreign language. Not knowing in what languages they were, I simply took pleasure in staring at the images of the words. In the streets, I picked up any papers with words. I cleaned the dust off and read whatever was there, or sometimes after the rains, I found papers in the mud and took them home and waited until they dried. Gradually, unfamiliar patterns of words had become familiar, their meanings clearer. Each linked to images and stories... I turned words over in my mind and silently recreated their sound.

My mother and father were so proud of me. My mother took me with her on shopping trips so that I could read her the use-by-date on cans such as sardines, tomatoes, salsa or Nido milk powder. My father let me read him and his friends the news from the papers every evening no matter what the date on the newspapers was.

At the age of 12, I went back to school, a year late. My teacher noticed how good I was at reading. Most of the people in the camp did not have radios but my teacher had one. He began transcribing the news from the radio at night so that I could read it to the students the next day. In the mornings, hundreds of students would line up for the morning queues, six classes lined up in rectangular form, 2 rows deep. I'd stand in the middle and read.

The first news broadcast I ever read out was:

> *Fifty naval force fighters from Eritrean People's Liberation Front completed a successful attack on Nacura prison camp in Dahlak archipelago. The camp was established by the former Italian colonial rulers and is now used by Ethiopian occupying forces to detain thousands of innocent Eritreans. The forces freed more than 500 prisoners and killed more than 30 enemy soldiers...*

SHE WAS SUPPOSED TO BE MY FIRST LOVE

She didn't hug me. She didn't kiss me on the cheek. She didn't shake my hand. I kept repeating these sentences to myself in no particular order while I lay in bed in the morning, having no reason to get up.

My cousin Romana had arrived last night. She was covered from head to toe in black fabric, her hands were in black gloves, and her feet were in black socks. She didn't say a word, just walked past me, head down. I had hardly slept for days thinking about her visit. Romana is about 15, only a few months younger than I am, and for one reason or another we hadn't seen each other for eight years. She and her mother, my aunt, will be staying with us for a few days. I don't know how I will cope with her presence in our flat, as the romantic thoughts I had of her prior to her arrival have yet to fade. And now I have to forget my imaginings of us talking and playing together. Romana is the only girl I have thought about since we left our village to come to this city. Her face was one of the last female faces I saw before I left. Since then, I haven't seen a young woman's uncovered face for more than 1835 days, and now it seems I will carry on counting.

I sat dejected on the living room sofa drinking tea. My father, mother, and aunt were talking; I hardly noticed them. Romana was alone in the guest room, I suppose eating her breakfast and drinking tea or perhaps a cup of hot milk.

Then she entered the living room, wearing a long black shawl and black gloves, with only her eyes and eyebrows visible. Everyone's head turned towards her. She handed me a package and I said: 'For me?'

Romana nodded. I smiled at her and opened the package; it was a long-sleeved white shirt; I was very happy.

I hurried to my room, took off my T-shirt and put on Romana's shirt, standing in front of the mirror. But the shirt was too tight. I fastened the buttons with much difficulty, my belly bursting out from beneath. All of a sudden, I remembered chewing gum. In our village, Romana and I were neighbours, and we always used to play together after school. Sometimes I used to buy her chewing gum with my pocket money. In our village, the older boys bought girls chewing gum if they wanted to seduce them. The girls loved chewing gum – I don't remember why but they loved it.

I ran back to the living room. Everyone laughed when they saw me, although perhaps not Romana.

'I love it. It's really nice,' I said, and as I was about to hug her to show my gratitude, Romana moved back, thrusting her right arm forward and trying to stop me with her hand. I stopped before she touched me but I wished I hadn't.

Later on, Romana informed me via my mother that she was not to speak to me nor I to her. I wasn't allowed to hear her voice or look at her. I was devastated. I couldn't understand why she came to visit us in the first place, if she didn't want to speak to me or show her face. I suppose I will have to wait another 1700 days to see a woman's face, that is to say until I get married. With a little luck, perhaps I will be able to see my bride's face before my wedding night.

I hated the city I lived in. I couldn't bear the traditions to which we, the foreigners, must adhere. I hated my parents too; I blamed them for bringing me to this city. I thought badly of them for being illiterate and believing in those traditions not only as if they were our own, but as if they had been ours for generations, to the point of separating men and women in our own house. When there is a celebration, for example, and people visit us, I show the women to the guest room and lead the men into the living room. I then make sure that the living room door, which is opposite the kitchen door and separated by the courtyard, is closed, so that if women happen to walk to the kitchen – and they often do – they can go through the courtyard without being seen by the men. And if a man wants to go the bathroom, I call out to the women to close the guest room and kitchen doors. I hated Romana's city even more than mine. I lamented her fanatical devotion to her adopted city's traditions and resented having to comply with these rules in my own house.

The next day, I decided to ignore Romana's request. I wrote her a note that I had copied from a magazine a week earlier. It said:

I, without you, am like a night without the moon,
a book without words and a pen without ink.

I hoped Romana would like those words. I hoped that they would soften her heart and that she might decide to see me in secret. I would then take her to the sea, we would walk side by side, or, if she liked, she could walk five metres behind me. And if she still wouldn't speak to me, then we'd enjoy the murmur of the sea or the sunset in silence.

My mother and aunt were in the kitchen. There was nobody in the living room or in the bathroom. So I assumed that Romana was in her room. I folded the note, put one red bubble gum ball, strawberry flavour, on top of it and slipped it underneath the door. I then knocked at the door and hurried back to my room, leaving my door open.

I waited. I waited for a long time. Nothing.

I hurried out of my room and tiptoed to the guest room, then went down on my knees and looked through the gap under the door. The note and the bubble gum weren't there. I could see Romana's bare feet: she wasn't moving; her toenails were painted green.

I walked back to my room.

I sat on my bed and buried my face in my hands. Romana's body, though it was covered, was driving me mad. My body had begun to feel different since she had come to our house. I got aroused whenever I saw her or she walked past me, and I wanted to touch her. I took a photograph out of my pocket that I'd been wanting to show Romana. The photograph was of Romana and me. I was very lucky to have that photograph. There's a boy at my school who swears he has never in his whole life seen a woman's face in the flesh. His mother died giving birth to him and with no female relatives, he grew up alone with his father. I am more fortunate. The photograph of Romana and me was taken when we were six or seven. We are standing next to each other and looking at the camera. I am wearing a sky blue T-shirt and yellow football shorts, Romana is wearing a pale pink dress that reaches just below her ankles. My left hand is behind my back and the other is holding Romana's left hand. I have a little smile on my face. Romana is smiling too, but her mouth is shut tight as if she's trying to stop herself from laughing out loud.

I stopped looking at the photograph and tried to imagine what Romana might look like now. Seeing her eyes, eyebrows and feet, I imagined her to be beautiful or at least attractive. I imagined her hair to be long and soft, her skin smooth and brown, her lips tender, her shoulders broad, her breasts large and her belly flat. I imagined her bottom to be big, her hips rounded and her legs slender.

I put the photograph aside and took a book from under my pillow. I opened it to a page marked by a bookmark, a small cut-out rectangular picture of a woman's leg. I got this cut-out from a school friend. This friend managed to get a picture of a foreign woman in a short skirt and a tight see-through T-shirt which revealed her big breasts underneath. Her legs were long and slim and she wore high heels. After weeks of begging, this friend agreed to cut out the left leg and give it to me. This was a real triumph for me as it was impossible for us young ones to get hold of the smuggled pornographic pictures and videos circulating; everything that has anything to do with women's bodies is strictly controlled by the city's authorities. On TV, for example, we are only allowed see women's faces and they are always foreigners. In newspapers and magazines, any photographs of women black out everything except the face.

I don't really read the book. I just look at its line drawings, almost every night. I found it under the spare bed in my room. I suspect it was left by one of my mother's relatives, Ibrahim. Ibrahim was a young man, probably in his late twenties, and he stayed with us for a few days. Once, in the middle of the night, I woke up to find Ibrahim sleeping behind me on my bed. As I was in a hurry to pee, I rushed to the bathroom. When I came back to my room I switched on the light to find Ibrahim asleep on the spare bed. Anyway, the book was written by a doctor and all about sex and health. What intrigued me were its anatomy drawings in the women's chapter, particularly the women's contours. There were only two positions: one standing, with the legs apart, and the other sitting, with the legs wide apart and a clear detailed drawing of the vagina. Whenever I looked at those drawings, I got aroused and my penis got erect. There was also a chapter about masturbation, what it is, how it is done and the pros and cons of doing it. I tried many times to do it, according to the instructions in the chapter. But I have never achieved the end result the way it was detailed in the book.

Now I locked my door and took my clothes off. Holding the book, I stood in front of the mirror. I gazed at the reflection of my naked body for a while. I looked at my penis and then at the line drawing - the standing posture. I tucked away my penis between my thighs and gazed at my reflection. I looked at the line drawing of the standing woman's vagina. I closed my eyes and tried to imagine Romana's but it was in vain. I went down on my knees and dropped the book. I lay on my side and closed my eyes.

Late in the afternoon, my mother and aunt were with Romana in the kitchen. I tiptoed into the courtyard and stood next to the kitchen door; it was ajar. I pinned my ear to the door and listened to their conversation.

'... You have to keep the heat high and stir every 3 to 5 minutes,' my mother was saying. 'Don't let the onion stick for too long to the pan otherwise it will taste burnt— Why are you laughing?' Romana must have laughed quietly, for I hadn't heard her. 'I don't know,' said Romana. 'I have been laughing all afternoon.'

'I usually put in a little bit of water so the onion won't stick to the pan,' said Aunt.

'You should never put water unless the onion gets too sticky otherwise you won't have a strong taste on the sauce. The chicken is...'

I tiptoed back to my room.

I took the photograph of Romana and me, put it in my pocket and left my room.

I knocked on the kitchen door and said, 'Can I come in?'

'Wait!' mum shouted.

A few moments later, mum shouted, 'Come in.'

I entered the hot kitchen. Mum and Aunt were sweating. Aunt was taking the skin off a whole chicken at the kitchen counter on my left, and on my right, Mum was standing in front of the oven stirring the onion in a large pan. Romana was standing next to mum, still wearing her long shawl. I saw her pulling her veil up closer to her lower eyelashes. I walked towards Romana, and as I got closer was struck by her eyebrows. They were black and thick and well trimmed. I thought for a moment about how she took care of her looks. There was no sweat on the visible uncovered area around her eyes. She must have dried it before I came in, I thought. I broke into a smile and showed Romana our photograph, pointing to her and me. Romana snatched the photograph from my hand, looked at it for a moment and cut it in half. She gave me the half where I am in the picture, tore the other half to pieces and threw them on the floor. Then she turned her head away. I got so incensed that I screamed and swore at her. When Romana heard my swearing, she put both hands on her covered ears while Mum and Aunt looked on. I picked up the pieces from the floor and went to my room.

I sat on my bed, trying to rearrange the fragments of the photograph and thinking of how to be cruel to Romana. I wanted to break her to pieces, to literally break her apart. I would also be careful so as to avoid the terrible punishment that I would get from my father, I thought. But then a sudden anger seized me and I left my room.

The kitchen door was still open; I went in and saw Mother peeling some boiled eggs. Aunt was talking to Romana and they were both were standing by the window. I said to my mother, 'Can I tell you something?'

'What, my dear?' mother said.

'Yesterday,' I said loudly, 'I was walking in the street and saw a woman sitting on the pavement. I thought she might be Romana. I went down to help her and she turned out be a goat.'

Mother immediately took one of her shoes off; I ran to my room and quickly locked the door. My mother followed me and pounded the door with her shoe before walking away.

I opened my door and tiptoed to the yard. I heard Romana crying while my mother and aunt tried to console her.

The next day, I wanted to say sorry to Romana in person, but since she wouldn't speak to me I couldn't. Still, I wouldn't forgive her for tearing up our photograph. Also, I could not stop thinking about what she had said: 'I don't know. I have been laughing all afternoon.' Why was she laughing all afternoon that day, all on her own in the guest room, I kept asking myself. God knows how I longed to see her face, her laughing face. I could have made her laugh more. I could have told her many jokes and funny stories.

While I was in the bathroom, I noticed the keyhole in the door. I peeped through it and thought of Romana. It's now or never, I told myself. Romana was leaving the next evening. Our bathroom had no shower curtains. It was the perfect way to finally see Romana's face and body before she went back to her city. So far, I had seen her feet and toenails, and her eyes. Through this keyhole, I wanted to see her face, hands, fingers, legs, thighs, buttocks, belly, breasts and nipples, arms, back, teeth, hair, and her pussy.

Later that morning, I saw Romana enter our bathroom. The keyhole, I said to myself. But the trouble was, my mother and aunt were in the kitchen and my father was in the living room. I stood motionless for a moment. I tiptoed towards the living room and stood by the open door. I saw Father's back: he was sitting on the sofa watching a sermon on TV. I tiptoed towards the kitchen and stopped by the door, half open: Mum and Aunt were cooking. I tiptoed towards the bathroom, shaking, my heart fluttering. I went down on my knees and peered through the hole. After no more than ten seconds, I felt a hand on my back; it was my father's. He dragged me by my collar to my room and closed the door. I swore to him that I had seen nothing. Father slapped my face with his right hand then with his left then with his right then with his left until I fell back onto the bed. I cried without making a sound. Father didn't say a word to me. He took out a rope from under my bed. He dragged me off the bed by my ear, tied my both hands together and then tied me to one of the bed legs. He left the room and closed the door behind him.

I lay on my back with tears were running down my face. But all I could think about was what I had seen. I had seen Romana's face in profile. I had seen her hair; it was long, curly and soft. I had seen her stroking her hair with both hands while looking at her reflection in the mirror. And as she was about to turn her head, perhaps towards me, I had felt my father's hand. I fell in love with the profile, and wished I had seen her face in its entirety. I wished I had delayed my decision to peep by just a few seconds or perhaps a minute, for then I might have seen her whole face or perhaps even her whole body.

And tomorrow she leaves, leaving me with only her profile, her curled hair, her feet and her words: 'I don't know. I have been laughing all afternoon.'

The first thing I did in the morning after my father untied me was to hurry to the bathroom to pee.

Later on, after much hugging and soothing from my mother – which I'd always get from her whenever my father punished me – I realised that my father had said nothing to her about the reasons for my punishment.

In the afternoon, I was sitting on my bed looking at my book and that little leg. I heard a sound outside the window. I got up and walked to the balcony, and saw Romana. The heat was intense. She was wearing her full black dress and standing outside the guest room's white balcony, looking down at the street. We lived on the second floor of a three storey apartment overlooking similar white apartments with almost identical balconies. The inhabitants rarely used their balconies.

'Romana!' I shouted.

Romana turned her head towards me, briefly.

'Romana, I love you' I said.

Romana turned her head towards me again. She stood still for a moment and then left the balcony and walked back to her room. I heard her closing the door. I laughed out loud, then went back to my room and threw myself on the bed, punching the mattress with my right hand and screaming, 'I hate you!'

Late in the afternoon, I was sitting on the sofa watching TV cartoons. With only her eyes visible, Romana was sitting with her mum on the sofa a few feet away from me. Then her mum left the room. I couldn't believe that we were alone together in a room at last. Romana seemed to have immersed herself in what we were watching and failed to notice that she was alone with me, or perhaps, I thought, she was enjoying the artificial flowers in the white vase on the coffee table. But then I saw her turn her head towards me. I saw her eyes stare at me, though only briefly. Then she carried on watching the cartoons. I felt she was waiting for me to say something. But I couldn't say a word. I don't know why but I couldn't say a word. Romana's right arm was bare from her elbow all the way to her fingers, as if she'd forgotten to cover her body. Her hand was resting on the arm of the sofa. Her fingers were brown and slender, with green painted fingernails. I stared. Her index finger was stroking the sofa's arm in a slow rhythm. I followed the movement of her finger wide eyed. All of a sudden, I remembered that this right hand had a history with my penis.

One night, I had been playing hide and seek in our village with Romana and a group of children, and I was the seeker. I had found her hiding behind a tree. We had hugged and laughed, and then Romana had played with my penis with her right hand.

As I looked at the hand again, an intense sensation overwhelmed me. My heart was pounding. I pressed my thighs against my penis. I felt it getting warmer. I put my left hand inside my trousers and my fingers felt its warmness. I closed my eyes and my mouth fell open I was breathing heavily. My lower jaw was shaking. I had never felt like this before. Then I realised I was wet with warm liquid. I breathed faster and faster. I rested my head against the arm of the sofa, looking at Romana's arm, and closed my eyes. Moments later, I opened my eyes and saw Romana standing over me. She was looking at my face and then turned her head towards my crotch. My hand was still inside my trousers. Suddenly, Romana ran away. I didn't care.

Ever since, I've carried on pressing my thighs together whenever I feel I like it, wherever I stand or lie or sit.

AN ACHE

There were three words. She uttered them as I stared at her back. She was wearing a blue blouse and a long dark skirt. Perhaps her hair was covered. It was in my dream. I often used to dream about my birthplace, but I have been away far too long and my village is too remote to matter to me. I had run away after losing my hearing. That is another story.

As I remembered my dream about this woman, I became convinced that it had actually taken place. And my deafness makes the memory of those three words significant. Now, apart from my daily struggle against tinnitus, with its ringing, buzzing, humming, grinding, hissing, whistling, sizzling and whooshing, nothing really happens in my life and so there is nothing much to tell apart from dreams and the past.

It was a long time ago, perhaps when I was nine or ten years old. It was inside a hut, when I could hear, that I heard those three words. And though I remember being someone who could hear for eleven years of my life, I've forgotten the words I used to hear, or perhaps I try not to remember. My hearing loss, though an unpleasant experience when it happened, now I try to remember it goes like this: I got ill; I went to bed; I slept for a long time; I woke up. Everything was silent.

I cannot recall her name, but I believe she was our neighbour, or perhaps a family friend. She was young and married, in her early twenties, and her husband had been away for a long time when she said those three words. In those days, many husbands in the village would vanish for years to work in cities, leave their women behind, alone. The women waited. The men sent gifts, letters and tape recordings. Perhaps some of the women were unfaithful. The temptation must have been there for them. There were many young poor men who stayed behind and couldn't afford to get married. Like the ones who worked on the wheat fields outside the village. With their muscular and well-toned bodies, they would have loved to fall in love. But it would have brought dire consequences on the women; the village was small.

The men ran the village. They bent the laws to whatever suited them. For instance, though it was illegal, they turned a blind eye to the prostitutes' quarter. This was on the outskirts of the village, frequented by men young and old, married and unmarried, rich and poor. The prostitutes had no family connections to the village.

The men left for one reason: money. They would return for one reason: their wives. Among those who returned was one with a bad back who smiled a lot to show off his pair of gold teeth. Another came back pious and started preaching from his house, and another came back without his right hand and opened a restaurant; there were many stories of men coming home.

Aaaahhh was her first word. But I suppose her Aaaahhh was a different kind of Aaaahhh!

In that faraway moonlit Summer sky, I carried a lantern and followed her footsteps in the dust. Inside, I stood with wide-open and wandering eyes, near a half-closed door. In that deep silence, I shone my lantern up towards the cone-shaped ceiling. The structure was supported by long bendy sticks tied tightly with rags and covered with grass matting. On the dusty empty floor, there were two single, blue metal-frame beds, of a kind that only affluent people could afford, opposite each other. She stood against the dark, muddy, curved wall in front of an open, brand new red Samsonite suitcase, ignoring my presence.as if I already was too familiar. The suitcase was full of new colourful clothes, white, pink, green and violet, perfumes, gold necklaces and earrings, a gold woman's watch, make-up, one pair of red and one pair of black high heels. There was also a brand new Sony single-tape cassette player with a cassette inserted, and a 6 pack of Duracell batteries. In a hurry, the woman put in the batteries, played the tape and listened as if she had not heard a man's voice for a long time. It was a man talking in a language that I could not understand.

Outside the hut, there were about two or three young men, one of them was lying on a wooden bed. I heard his clear, youthful voice as he told an unremarkable story.

The woman stopped playing the tape and stood there, immobile, as if she was looking at the men through the wall. Then she tilted her head slowly to the right. She listened. I listened. All I could see, against the light of that single candle, were the visible lines of her long curled hair and the contours of her body, which gave infinite possibilities to my childish imagination.

The man got off the bed. We heard the straining ropes against the bed's wooden frame. He said, 'Aaaaah, what backache,' with a kind of groan as though he was stretching.

The woman stretched her back and slowly lifted her hands up in the air. She said three words, 'Aaaahhhh, what cuntache.'

THE RETURN OF THE FATHER

1

I sat alone in my courtyard, wearing blue and white striped pyjama trousers and a white vest, late on Friday night, enjoying the calm and the cool air after a hot summer's day. The courtyard was lit by a lantern next to a glass and a bottle of Arak on a small table. While sipping my third glass, I reminded myself to be careful not to get drunk tonight as I would be taking my son to his first swimming lesson in the river early in the morning. I enjoy these moments of the night. It is on these rare occasions that I can think about my worries. Lately, I have started to develop signs of irritation and distress whenever I look down or touch my waistline. From time to time, I measure it. It was about 108cm last week. I was alarmed. It was only 97cm a month ago. I don't have time to do any running or push-ups, as I am now working overtime so I can feed my son well. I have also begun to look at the mirror a lot these days. Not necessarily to look at my face, but trying in vain to count how much hair I have lost, or if I can find any new white ones. I have already discovered four or five on the left side of the back of my head. Three problems at once!

I looked at my watch: midnight. I closed my eyes in satisfaction as if I had solved all my problems. I usually feel like this when the liquor takes effect. But then I heard footsteps echoing outside the yard. I opened my eyes and listened carefully as the sound grew louder and nearer.

The courtyard door, which had no keys or locks, sprung wide open, and before I could do anything, a figure in a white shirt and dark-grey trousers had advanced and stopped in front of me. I got up and looked at him. He was tall – a good two inches taller than I am. He was silent. His gaze was fixed on my face and his eyes looked at me as if they already knew me.

I picked up the lantern, took a step back, and looked at him. He was a middle-aged man, perhaps in his late fifties or early sixties. He had a well-trimmed white moustache and thinning white hair. I tried to ignore my fears and asked, 'Who are you?'

'Birhan,' said the man, calmly.

'Yes,' I said.

'I am your father,' said the man and smiled.

The words shot into my ear like a bolt. I looked at him from head to toe while absorbing my shock. Then I shone the lantern closer to his face. I observed it with a great care: eyes, eyebrows, nose, lips, cheeks, ears. I moved further back and looked at his face again. Suddenly, I remembered my mother's words: you look like your father.

I fell to my knees and hugged the man's legs. He caressed my head gently and rubbed his hands through my hair; it felt good. I went on hugging him for a long time.

I brought my father a chair and a glass. He sat opposite

me. Although I could not remember ever using the words father or papa, I couldn't resist the urge to use them now. Not necessarily out of respect for my father – though I do respect him or at least his memory, but to see how would I feel about them. I thought for a moment and then said, 'Would you like a drink, father?'

I felt a strange sensation upon uttering the word.

'Never thought my son would be a drinker like me,' said Father and smiled.

'I don't drink that much, papa,' I said.

I noticed my father's quick glance towards me as I uttered the word papa. Personally, I couldn't tell the difference between the two words: Father or papa. My son calls me papa and I have heard him say the word father sometimes when talking to others about me. But I no longer remember how it felt at the beginning when he used those words.

I poured Arak into my father's glass. Father picked up the glass and drank it all at once. I poured another one and he drank it all at once again and smiled at me. I noticed that the light from the lantern fell on the left side of his face and made it look deformed. I moved the lantern to the middle of the table and said, 'I thought you were dead.'

'I was fighting in the war, son. We have won it now, after all those years. I hope history will remember us, us, the ones who scarified their souls and shed their blood to defeat the evil enemy and free our country to give birth to a new nation.' He spoke in a clear, sharp voice.

Father looked calm and strong, yet I could see he was exhausted; his eyes looked tired. I poured more Arak into my father's glass and scrutinized his face again while he drank. He had an oval-shaped face; his forehead was broad and wide with three deep wrinkles running across it; his eyebrows were mostly white and his jet-black pupils reflected the light of the lantern; his head was small, making his bald spot seem bigger that it actually was; his neck was short but proportionate to his head and shoulders; his cheeks had a few small wrinkles, divided unevenly on both cheeks; yet he seemed really handsome. I wondered whether this was what I might look like when I reached his age; I thought I wouldn't have minded that at all. Soon, my thoughts turned to my son and how I have always had a feeling of nostalgia towards my childhood when I look at him. Many people liken him to me and say he has my eyebrows, nose, lips and smile. I have always wondered if I looked like my son when I was at his age. I don't have any photographs of my childhood.

I offered my father a cigarette. He took it, and before I could light it for him, I touched, then briefly held his right hand. My father looked at me, I didn't know if it was a look of appreciation or wonder. His hand was warm and his palm was calloused, his fingers were long and slender.

I took a cigarette for myself and lit them both with a match. I exhaled after taking a puff and asked, 'How did you find me, Father?'

'After the liberation I went immediately to our hometown. I looked for you and your mother and I was told you might be here,' said father, as if he was relieved. 'How is everything?'

I looked at my father's upper body. His arms were strong and his shoulders broad. I said, 'I have a wife and a four-year-old son.'

'Oh! I am a grandfather!' Father jumped from his seat and thanked God, throwing both hands up in the air. 'I have been dreaming about this day from the day I left you, and during all my battles and victories. I have always thought my son will be his father's son; will get married and give me a grandchild. I spent thirty years of my life fighting for the future of a new country for you and my grandson. It is a new beginning for us and all our countrymen. I came all this way to take you all back home.' My father clenched his fist. 'Your liberated new home!'

I leaned back in my chair and let my arms hang down. I looked away and tried to ignore everything for a moment. Then I felt a sudden drunken clarity. I sighed deeply 'Father,' I said, 'I love my son like a father without having had the experience of being loved like a son.'

Father closed his eyes as if a knife had sliced through his heart. We both drank from our glasses, saying nothing for a while. I poured more drink into my father's glass and broke the silence. 'I was four years old when you left. I have never been able to remember your face. The only thing I remember is mum kissing you uncontrollably on your head, neck and feet before you left...'

'No, no... Your mum wasn't kissing me,' Father interrupted. 'She was begging me not to leave. She was dragging me by my neck, waist and feet. I had to leave because I killed someone in our local café. He insulted my family and me. I put a bullet in his head. The next day, his whole clan was after me. I had no choice but to leave. I went to the mountains and got lost. Then, by chance, I found some resistance fighters. They helped me and fed me. And convinced me to join them.' My father shrugged his shoulders. 'I had no choice.'

'After you left, mother and I went to see auntie. We stayed at auntie's house...'

'Where is she now?' interrupted father.

'Two years ago, she went to visit auntie and got stuck in the fighting...'

'Have you heard from her?'

'She will be back soon...'

'Ah,' father interrupted, burying his face in his hands, 'I thought many times to escape and return, just to see you and your mother. But the situation was becoming more complicated by the day. I was young and fearless and killed many enemies and saved many comrades. Soon I was made a sergeant, I had a group of young fighters under my command, and I found it very difficult to desert them.'

'I used to cry whenever the teachers in my school asked us to bring in our fathers to discuss something important,' I said. 'Mum made ends meet. Then came the siege. After a year of being under attack almost every night by resistance fighters, we left the city—'

'I was a first lieutenant then,' father interrupted. 'I led a special force to oversee a highly classified operation. We entered the city in darkness. We stayed there for a few days. I wish I knew you were there.'

'We crossed the country by foot and on camels. Later, we heard that the rebels advancing on the capital had been defeated—'

My father suddenly stood and pointed his finger at me, shouting, 'Defeated! We weren't defeated! We retreated because the occupying enemy had acquired new advanced weapons from foreign countries. We were left alone. Nobody helped us. I was ordered to withdraw my unit in order to save the civilians from a certain bloodbath.'

I looked at my father while he was standing and then at his big belly. How odd, I thought, for a foot soldier to look like this. My father sat down and drank from his glass. I drank from mine, and said, 'I have been working in a shop for uncle Yousif...'

'Uncle! You have never had an uncle,' interrupted father.

'No, no… he is an old man. Everyone here calls him uncle Yousif. He is nice and caring.'

'Who is this uncle?' said father, after a short pause.

'He came here when civil war was raging between the rebels—'

'It was not a civil war!' father shouted. 'It was just a treacherous drunkard who rejected unity and led a few rebels astray from their original ideals. We defeated them and corrected their ways in the end. Look at us, we are all one united people now.' My father looked at his glass and then at me. I poured more Arak into his glass. He drank a shot, calmed down, and said, 'Tell me who is this… uncle?'

'Everybody here calls him uncle Yousif because he is so generous with his money and very kind—'

'And what has he done for you?' father interrupted.

'As an orphan, he acted—'

'Orphan!' shouted father.

'Father, everybody thought you were dead. Nobody ever heard anything from you,' I said in a gentle tone, trying to calm him.

'And what has he done for you, anyway?'

'Uncle Yousif appointed me as an assistant shopkeeper in his shop. Uncle Yousif has the biggest shop here. A few years later he promoted me to manager.'

'And what else has he done for you?'

'A few years ago, uncle Yousif begged me to get married and settle down. At first I refused but he reasoned with me and convinced me how marriage would be good for me. He found me a good woman, Mebrat. He asked for her hand on my behalf and was a witness to the wedding.'

Father shook his head. He poured more Arak into his glass

and drank a shot, and then took a cigarette and lit it. Father took several drags in succession, looked at me for a moment, and said, 'Have you heard about our final battle?'

'Of course, father,' I said, smiling. 'Everybody here celebrated it—'

'It was the greatest battle in our history,' father interrupted. 'We destroyed the enemy's main base. It lasted three nights and four days. I was a colonel. I led six battalions. We killed thousands and thousands of enemy soldiers. Can you imagine thousands and thousands of dead men and not a space left bare on the ground to step on. In this battle, the enemy lost whole divisions of its best-trained and armed troops. They left behind a weapons stockpile they had amassed to carry out what they believed was to have been 'a decisive offensive' against us, but we outwitted them. It was in this battle we made the enemy cut off his own right hand with his left hand. This battle opened all the doors for us to finally liberate our country from the evil enemy!'

'I had my son at that time. At his birth, uncle Yousif raised my son high up in the air—'

'He was at his birth!' father interrupted.

'Yes and named him—'

'He named him! He named my grandson!'

My father stood up and poured more Arak into his glass. He picked up the glass and walked around slowly, then downed his glass and said, 'Whatever could have happened for things to have come to this?' He sat down and murmured, 'Whatever... Happened... From... To this... This way.'

I suspected my father was drunk. The strength I had felt in him earlier had now disappeared into his drunken eyes and mouth. He was sad and slurring his words as he spoke. I couldn't understand my father's reaction. In a way, I was satisfied with my life. Besides, I was drunk too.

I looked at the bottle; it was empty. I got up and said, 'We need another bottle, father.'

My father looked at me and nodded. I picked up the empty bottle.

'Father, I have often asked myself: What could have happened?'

'What could have happened?' Father repeated, looking at me.

'What would have happened if you had never gone away?' I said and walked away.

I came back with another bottle of Arak. My father had a distant look in his eyes. He was shaking his head and murmuring, 'Only... If only... Whatever... If...?'

I sat down and I poured more Arak into our glasses. We both downed them. My father looked at me with his dreamy, slumbering eyes. I suspected my eyes were no different. I poured more Arak into our glasses, and said, 'Let's think about what could have happened.'

'And forget what happened,' said father.

'There is nothing to forget. Nothing happened between us... Well, apart from those four years I don't remember.'

'I mean forget what happened while we were apart.'

'It doesn't concern us,' I said. 'Let's just start anew. Let's live all that time we missed in real time.'

'How?'

'We will start to act like a father and son, starting from the day you departed. I will be a four year-old boy and you—'

'What about the future?'

'Forget the future. Let's live the past from tomorrow.'

'What about my grandson and your wife?'

'Forget them.'

'But I want to be a grandfather too.'

'No. All my life I dreamt of having a father. You and I will live our lives as we would have always wanted them to be.'

My father stood up holding his glass. I followed suit. 'Tomorrow shall be our new past, then,' said father.

'Now we will rehearse for tomorrow,' I said.

'Rehearse?'

'Yes, we will rehearse part of our missed past.'

2

The son screams loudly and runs around the yard, arms flailing. He then runs towards his father who is sitting on a chair, and jumps onto his lap. The son screams with his mouth wide open, kisses his father's forehead and pinches his cheeks with both hands. 'Papa! Papa! Papa!' he shouts.

The father looks at his son with curiosity. Then the chair creaks and collapses under their weight. The son lands on his father and his father lets out a groan. Their faces are inches apart and they stare at each other. The son is disappointed with his father's lack of involvement. He slowly gets up off his father and pours him another glass.

'Father!' he says. 'You need to relax.'

The son drinks a shot from the bottle and offers the glass to his father. The father takes the glass and props himself up against the wall. The son jumps up and down and then walks to his father. He stops in front of him and asks, 'How old are you, papa?'

'Fifty six,' answers the father.

'You are fifty six, papa!'

'Yes.'

The son counts with his fingers. 'One, two, three, four, five, six, seven, eight, nine, ten, eleven, twenty, twenty three, forty, thirty five, forty five, forty seven, forty six, forty eight, forty nine, fifty, fifty two, fifty five, fifty three, fifty five, fifty six... Fifty six! You are fifty six, papa!"

'Yes,' says the father.

'I am four, papa. You are fifty six!'

'Yes,' says the father. 'No, no.' He pauses. 'I am twenty six.'

The son counts again with his fingers. 'Twenty six, papa!'

'Yes,' says the father.

The son once again runs around the yard and comes to a standstill before his father. He lets out a scream near his father's face and begins making faces and grimacing before bursting into tears. The father says, 'Stop crying, son,' in a distant voice.

The son stops crying and his expression becomes serious. 'Father!' he says. 'I know you have been away fighting, but haven't you ever seen how a child behaves? Don't you remember the times we had together? Have we ever played together?'

The father goes into deep reflection for a moment, and says, 'I used to carry you on my shoulders.'

The son smiles with dreamy, faraway eyes and says, 'Really!'

The father nods with a smile. 'And we used to play football together.'

'Really! I used to play for my local team, Father,' says the son.

'What position?'

'I was a winger.'

'I used to play as an attacker,' the father laughs. 'Maybe

in the future we should play in the same team. You supply the crosses, I score the goals.'

The father and son laugh out loud for a while.

All of the sudden, the father stops laughing, stares down at the ground and closes his eyes. The son looks at his father. The father looks lost in his thoughts. The son shakes his father by his shoulders. The father opens his eyes, and says, 'What?'

'Father! Father! We need to rehearse.'

The son begins to walk around the yard with his hands around his back. He starts to jump up and down and shouts, 'Papa! Papa! You are a donkey.'

'A donkey?' asks the father.

'Papa. Papa be a donkey, papa... I want to ride on your back, papa,' says the son.

'Ah!' says the father and goes down on all fours.

The son climbs on his father's back. Holding his father's collar with one hand, the son slaps his father's backside with the other hand and shouts, 'Go, papa! Go! Go!'

The father begins to crawl slowly on his hands and knees. The son gets off his father's back and asks his father to stand. The son goes down on all fours and asks the father to watch him as he crawls quickly on all fours around the yard. 'Like this,' he says to his father.

The father nods. The son stands, and says, 'Lets do it again.'

The father goes down on all fours. The son climbs on his father's back and holds him by his collar. He then slaps his father's backside repeatedly, and shouts, 'Let's go, papa! Go! Go!'

The father crawls quickly.

'How old are you, papa?' the son shouts.

'Twenty six,' says the father.

'Papa, twenty six.'

The son gets off his father's back and runs toward a tree in the yard, then stops and gazes at its branches and leaves. The father looks at his son and then at the tree. The son begins to climb the tree. After a laborious struggle with his belly, the son manages to move up and disappear into a mass of leaves. The son lies on his belly, straddling a branch and hugging it with both arms.

The father picks up the lantern and looks for his son through the tree leaves. 'Where are you, Birhan?' he shouts 'Where are you?'

'Here papa!'

'Are you ok?'

'I am scared, papa.'

'Please come down.'

'Help me, papa! Help me, papa!'

'Wait there. Wait!'

The father puts the lantern down away from the tree. The branch is starting to break under his son's weight. The son loses his grip and starts to fall. His father stretches out his arms to catch him. The son falls, still holding the branch, comes hurtling towards his father and lands on him. The branch hits the father on the head. They both remain motionless. The son slowly gets up and realises that his father's forehead is bleeding. The son tries to help his father sit up, but the father struggles to do so as he has damaged his hip and his left arm is twisted underneath him. The son touches his father's head and says, 'Papa, papa, papa.'

'Oh! Oh... oh,' moans Father. 'Get me some scissors.'

The son runs off and returns with a pair of scissors. The father asks his son to cut both sleeves of his shirt. The son, instead of cutting the sleeves, begins to cut his father's shirt, starting from the hemline while shouting, 'Papa! Papa!'

'Cut the sleeves! I said cut the sleeves!' shouts the father.

The son cuts the sleeves. With one of the sleeves, the son makes a makeshift sling for his father's broken arm, and instead of bandaging his father's head with the other sleeve, he tries to bandage his father's mouth. At that point his father shouts, 'Stop it! Stop it!'

The son stops. After a moment, he bandages his father's head with the remaining sleeve and helps him sit up. 'Shall we stop the rehearsal now, Father?' he asks.

'Do you want to, son?'

'I don't mind, but it is up to you, Father.'

The father looks at the branch and then at his son, and says, 'No, let's carry on.'

'Ok, if that is what you want, Father,' says the son.

'Yes,' says the father. 'Are you sure, son?'

'Yes, Father.'

The son helps his father to his feet. The father, still in obvious pain, asks his son to take one of the smaller branches off the larger broken branch and clean off the leaves. The son obeys. The father takes the branch and orders his son to get down on all fours. The son looks at his father and then at the stick and shouts, 'Papa! Papa! Papa!'

'Get down on your knees and hands. Get down!' shouts the father.

The son goes down on all fours, and looks up at his father. The father starts to hit his son hard on his bottom. The son screams and cries out, 'Papa! No papa, don't hit me papa. Papa! Papa!'

The father stops hitting the son immediately. The son looks up at his father, and says, 'You shouldn't stop, Father.

You hit a child, pain or no pain, he will scream anyway. You should stop when you feel it is enough.'

The father nods slowly and begins to hit the son very hard. The son screams, and cries out, 'Papa! Papa! Papa! Papa!'

The father carries on hitting the son ferociously on his bottom and his back till the son can no longer bear it. Almost in tears, the son gets up while rubbing his bottom and his back with both hands. The father looks at his son for a while, and says, 'Do you want to do it again, son?'

The son shakes his head. He drinks from the bottle and pours another shot into his father's glass. The son takes out a cigarette for himself and one for his father and lights them. The son takes a puff, and shouts, 'I want to go to school, papa.'

'To school! Now?' protests the father while looking at his watch.

'I want to go to the school, papa.'

'It is too late now.'

The son begins to cry loudly. 'I want to go to school, papa. Papa! I want to go to school.'

'Ok, ok,' says the father.

The son stops crying and carries on smoking. Moments later, he picks up the lantern and the bottle and hands the lantern to his father. The father holds the lantern with his right hand and limps along; his drunkenness seems to ease the pain.

It is a starry night. The streets are deserted. The houses are silent. Father and son soon approach a Y-junction. The son looks around and points to a narrow street. After a few minutes of walking, they find themselves in front of a slope. The son looks down at the slope and shakes his head. 'No, not this way, Father.'

They double back onto the street and head to the junction they had crossed earlier. The son points towards another narrow street. After some time, they reach a dry, muddy field. They cross the field and stop. The son takes the lantern from his father, walks slowly and shines the lantern upward, revealing a yellow brick wall. He walks to a worn, rusty metal door which is locked. The son pounds on the door, crying out, 'The school is closed, papa. The school is closed.'

'Of course it is. It is night time, son,' says the father.

The son walks past two closed windows; one is dark green and the other plain and rusty. The son goes into a small hall through an open rectangular entrance. Inside are two closed rusty metal doors opposite each other. The son rattles each one and cries, 'But I want to go to school, papa.'

'The school is closed,' says the father.

'I want to go school, papa. This not right, papa.'

'What do you want me to do? The school is closed. It is night time!'

The son carries on crying and screaming. 'I want go to school! This isn't fair.'

The father sits down against the wall and signals to his son to sit down. The son sits next to his father, still crying, and puts the lantern down.

'Come on, my child, you are just drunk,' soothes the father.

'I am not drunk!' yells the son, 'I am a child, Father.'

The father hugs his son and caresses his hair. The son soon stops crying. The son takes out a cigarette for himself and one for his father.

After some time, they leave from the school. All of a sudden, the son stops, and shouts, 'Poo! Poo! I want to poo, papa.'

'What? Here?'

The son squats down with his trousers round his ankles. Once he has finished, he shouts, 'Papa! Papa!'

'What now?' says the father.

'Papa! Wipe me, papa,' pleads the son.

'What!' says the father. He shines the lantern down and sees some rocks on the ground. He picks out some smooth rocks and proceeds to wipe his son's bottom. As soon as the father finishes, the son jumps up and pulls up his trousers. The son then drinks a shot of Arak and hands the bottle to his father. The father drinks a shot, and asks, 'For how long are we going to do this?'

The son looks at his watch briefly and says, 'This year, I will be four years old for one year, father. Next year I will be five. The year after, I will be six then seven, eight, nine...'

'Ok! Ok! I get it,' interrupts the father and shakes his head.

'Are you twenty six, papa?' asks the son.

'Yes! Yes! Yes!'

The son, still holding the bottle, takes the lantern from his father, walks away and stops at the edge of a deep dry riverbed. The riverbed is flat and wide enough for more than two people to walk through it next to each other. The son jumps down into it. He looks up at his father, then runs at breakneck speed on its dry, smooth soil and scattered rocks, while shouting, 'Catch me, papa! Catch me!'

The father jumps down, moans and limps along after the lantern's glow. After some time, the son halts and puts the lantern down. He falls to his knees, and then lies on his back against the riverbed bank. The father reaches him some time later and also falls to the ground. He takes the lantern from his son and shines it nearer to his son's face, staring at him with unfriendly eyes. The son laughs out loud and drinks from the bottle and passes it to his father. They both take turns swigging from the bottle.

'Are you twenty six, papa?' asks the son, laughing.

'I swear to God if you ask me about my age again, I will kill you,' shouts the father.

The son begins to cry loudly. The father looks at his son, and says, 'I am sorry! I am sorry, my child. I didn't mean it.'

The father moves closer to his son, hugs and kisses him on his cheeks and forehead. He gently touches his cheek and smiles at him. The son stops crying and puts his head on his father's shoulder. The father closes his eyes and takes a few deep breaths. He smiles to himself and opens his eyes. He takes out a cigarette and asks his son to light it for him. The son lights his father's cigarette and puts his head back on his father's shoulder. Before he inhales, the father says, 'Son, look. Look.'

As the son looks on the father tries to blow smoke rings without success. The son takes the cigarette from his father's mouth and blows perfect smoke rings, saying, 'Papa, papa! I can do it.'

After some time, they move out of the riverbed. The father limps along holding the lantern whilst the son staggers next to him holding the bottle. The father spots a tree nearby, walks over to it and says, 'Come on, my child. I will carry you on my shoulders.'

The son walks over, grasping the bottle. Using the tree trunk as a support, the son climbs up onto his father's shoulders. The father, holding the lantern, lifts him up with some difficulty and limps along. The son drinks a shot, and says, 'Papa. Papa. Let's go to the river.'

'What? Now?' asks the father. 'Ok! Ok!'

'Papa! You are so nice. I love you so much,' says the son.

'Oh! Thank you. Thank you. I love you so much too, my dear child.'

The son kisses his father's bald spot and rests his head on it for a while. The son then takes out two cigarettes, puts one in his mouth and the other into his father's. The father stops. The son lights the cigarettes and they both smoke.

They enter a dusty ridge carved out of rock, its rough surface looking dark brown under the glow of the lantern. Then they walk into a steep sloping pass. The son drinks from the bottle and spits on his father's bald spot. The father shouts, 'Stop it!'

The son stops spitting at his father, and asks, 'Why do you have a big belly, papa?'

The father laughs and stops for a moment. 'When we liberated your country, my son, we didn't liberate it all in one burst. We liberated it tree by tree, street by street, village by village and town by town. You see, my boy, three years ago we liberated a small town and our brigade was stationed there. We stayed there for two years and we didn't do any fighting at all. The town was famed for its food and drink. The townsfolk liked us a lot. They would give us their best food and let us drink for free all the time...'

The son rubs his father's bald spot. He pats it softly, and then slaps it hard repeatedly, until the father says, 'Stop it!'

They reach the top of the pass and walk down the slope to reach the river. The son climbs off his father's shoulders. He drinks from the bottle and passes it to his father. The father sits down on the ground. The son's head spins from the swig he took. He begins to undress and strips down to his underwear. 'Papa! Papa! Teach me to swim.'

'I can't,' says the father.

'Why not?'

'Because I don't know how to swim.'

The son takes the lantern, walks to the riverbank and stops at the edge. He shines the lantern upward then downward and stares at the river.

'Be careful, my child. There might be a snake in the river,' warns the father

'No father! There was one last year and we killed him.'

'Good. Just be careful, my child.'

'How old are you, papa?'

'Twenty-six. I am twenty six,' shouts the father. 'What would you like to be when you grow up, son?' he asks.

'I want to be a driver, papa. I want to drive a car. I want a car, papa,' says the son.

'I want you to be a general. A general in our army.'

'Stop thinking about the war, father. You are a civilian now.'.

After struggling with his bruised arm, the father clasps his hands together and fashions a wind instrument. He blows into a small hole between his thumbs. Using his right hand and clasped fingers as air valves, he manages to mimic a rudimentary trumpet. The son enjoys the sounds his father is making and says, 'Papa! That is nice, papa.'

Upon his son's encouragement, the father carries on playing with his clasped hands for a while, and then says, 'This feels so good, my child. I wish I had never left you. I wish I didn't kill that man.'

'You didn't leave. You didn't kill anyone. Nothing has happened, Father,' says the son.

'I wish it was like that.'

'You didn't kill anybody, Father,' says the son. 'You just threatened to kill me a short time ago.'

'You are worried about something I didn't mean,' says the father, 'I killed someone for real, thirty years ago.'

'Father, you can't remember those thirty years, otherwise our deal will not work.'

The son walks back to his father and looks to his right side. He sees a slope. The son picks up the lantern and walks up the slope, stopping by a cliff. He shines the lantern down and looks at the river for a while. Then he goes back to his father. He puts the lantern down and sits on the ground. The son looks at his father and says, 'I want to play a game, papa! I want to play, papa!'

The father stops playing with his hands, and asks, 'What game do you want to play?'

The son thinks for a moment. 'Let's do wrestling, papa.'

'In this state?' the father cries out, looking at his broken arm.

'I want to wrestle, papa! I want to wrestle, papa!' shouts the son.

'Are you crazy or drunk? I can't wrestle like this.'

'I am not drunk. I am not crazy.' The son thinks for a moment. 'I am a child, Father.'

'I am tired, my dear child. Besides, I feel pain in my arm,' says the father.

The son begins to cry loudly. 'You aren't my father, papa. I love uncle Yousif, papa.'

'I am your father, like it or not,' shouts the father 'I fucked your mother and that is why you are here.'

The son stands up, and shouts back, 'Don't you ever talk about my mother like that, Father! She could have had a hundred lovers better than you if she had wanted to.'

The father stands up and glares at his son.

'She may have had two or three lovers—' the son says.

The father charges towards his son. He grabs his son's neck with his right hand and trips him with one of his legs. The son falls flat on his back. The father jumps over his son's belly, sits on it and grabs him by his neck, saying, 'So you want to wrestle, do you?'

The son tries to free himself from his father's grasp. 'This is a rehearsal, Father,' he says. 'This is a rehearsal.'

The son grabs his father's bruised left arm with both hands and tries to twist it. The father grasps some dust from the ground and throws it into his son's face. The son lets go of his father's arm. 'My eyes! My eyes!' he cries, wiping the dust off his face, 'I can't see.'

The father gets off his son's belly, moaning aloud in pain. The son sits, still wiping the dust off his face. The father manages to stand up with great difficulty, still moaning. He walks closer to his son and strokes his head, saying, 'Come on, wash your face, my child.'

The son gets up. The father, holding his son's hand, helps his son walk down to the riverbank. At the river bank, the son washes his face and says, 'I am fine, papa.'

They walk back and sit near the lantern. The son picks up the bottle of Arak and takes a swig, then hands the bottle to his father, who does the same.

'I have a better idea,' says the father.

'What?'

'A better game,' says the father, 'I'll sit down on my knees and you jump over my head. Then you sit down on your knees and I'll jump over yours, and so on.'

'That is a good game, papa. Let's play, papa,' says the son.

The father sits on his knees with his back to the river. But the son asks his father to change direction, facing the slope towards the cliff, which the father does. The son runs and jumps over his father's head. The son shouts in excitement and then sits a few feet away from his father. The father gets up and says, 'Son, when you are jumping over my head, shout: WHUP!'

The son nods. The father walks back a few metres, then runs, still limping, and shouts as he jumps over his son, 'WHUP!'

The father lands on his feet and moans in pain, then sits on his knees, still moaning.

And so it goes on, until the father jumps and lands in the river.

The father comes to the surface and thrashes his arms against the water in panic. He screams loudly, and shouts, 'Help! Help! Help me, my child! I can't swim... Help!'

The son doesn't move.

The father continues to shout, 'Help! Help!... Birhaa!... Birhaaaaaan!... Birhaaaa!'

Abrupt silence follows.

The son stands up and takes a few steps back, then falls to the ground. He then crawls on all fours and makes his way to the lantern. He picks up the lantern and stands up. He walks up the slope and stops at the edge. The son then lies down on his belly, shines the lantern down and looks into the river. He sees nothing but fast-moving water. 'Papa! Papa! Papa!' the son shouts.

There is no reply.

3

Dawn came. It was silent apart from the river's rattling currents.

Birhan was asleep near the edge of the cliff, curled into a

ball. Beside him was the lantern with its extinguished flame.

Birhan woke up with a heavy hangover. He stood up tiredly and was surprised to find himself in his underwear. He looked at his watch: 6:11 AM. He looked around: he was alone and felt confused.

Birhan picked up the lantern, walked down the slope and stopped. He was again surprised to see his clothes, an empty bottle, cigarettes and matches on the ground amongst the dust. Birhan stood still for a moment, then put the lantern down. He put his hands on his hips and looked at the river, then turned to look in the opposite direction: there were a few bush trees over a slope. Birhan looked down at the ground, trying to find footprints. But he couldn't see anything apart from the dull yellowish-brown dust and small rocks scattered around.

Birhan walked back to the edge of the cliff and stood still for a moment. He held his nose with his fingers and jumped, legs first, into the river. Birhan's feet popped out of the water, then disappeared for a long time. Then his head bobbed up. He slowly swam to the middle of the river and stopped; he turned his head left and right, looking at both riverbanks.

Birhan swam slowly towards the riverbank where his clothes were. Once he reached the shallow waters, he stopped swimming and walked out of the river. He brushed off the water from his head and body with his hands and put his clothes and his sandals on. He looked up the slope towards the cliff for a moment, then at the river.

Birhan took out a cigarette and opened the box of matches; there was only a single match left; he struck it. As he was trying to light the cigarette, the wind blew out the flame. Birhan threw the cigarette and the match to the ground. He picked up the lantern and walked away.

THE BRIDE

I was at my friends' house for dinner when I was first made aware of the rumour. On hearing it, I half laughed. But then memories of the wedding started to come back to me.

I protested to my friends A & V in front of the two other guests sitting at the dinner table – a couple I hadn't met before – saying, 'I didn't try to kiss the bride.' I took a quick gulp from my glass. 'It was an idea that came to me in a split second, to playfully separate the bride and groom for just a moment. I don't know for what reason... But when I saw them dancing on the dance floor, I stood between them and danced facing the bride.'

A & V looked at me, and A said, 'The bride herself told us you tried to kiss her.'

'Yeah!' V nodded.

I looked at the guests; I felt uncomfortable. 'I didn't try to kiss her,' I repeated. 'I just danced with her.'

'Do you remember when her cousin pulled you away?' said A, looking me directly in the eye.

'Yes, I remember. I didn't want to cause any trouble so I walked away.'

A & V eyed one other.

'Believe me! I didn't try to kiss her. I've never fancied her, anyway,' I said.

'You were drunk,' said V.

'I wasn't that drunk... listen, if I can remember what happens then I am not drunk. If I cannot remember what happens then I am drunk.' Afterwards, I decided to forget about the whole thing. The bride and groom had moved abroad, and I doubt I thought much of the incident or the dinner since then.

One day, my friend G, whom I hadn't seen or heard from for a long time, rang me and asked, 'Is it true?'

'What?' I said.

'That you tried to kiss the bride?'

'No! It isn't true!' I shouted.

'Tell me what happened,' G said.

I told G my version of events.

'Are you still friends?' G asked.

'Yes,' I said. 'I saw the bride and groom again two days after the wedding and there were hugs, smiles and laughter. She and the groom never mentioned the incident to me, and as far as I know we are still friends.'

Months later, I was at V's house for a drink. V handed me a book I had lent the bride some time before her wedding. I was surprised to learn that the groom had been to town to visit A & V.

As our night drew to a close, I said to V, 'I have a feeling the groom doesn't like me.'

'Are you surprised?' said V. 'You tried to kiss his wife.'

One afternoon, I was walking down the street and passed a pub. Inside, I saw a bride in her white dress, holding a glass of champagne. She was leaning against a dark brown bar stool, talking and laughing, surrounded by many guests.

I hurried past.

Suddenly, I saw the bride and the groom kiss each after their civil marriage ceremony. I remembered having our pictures taken with all the other guests outside on the stairs and against the backdrop of the white town hall. There I told the groom how good he looked. He was standing next to his mother, wearing a white and blue striped jacket, white trousers, a white shirt and blue tie. I saw his mum look at him as she heard my words, and saw the pride in her. I remembered that during lunch I had asked the bride how she felt about the ring on her finger, and she had answered, 'It hasn't sunk in yet.' I then saw her dancing under strobe lights with the groom. I saw a big arm dragging me away. I heard a man say, 'Leave them alone.' I wanted to shout no! This isn't true. It isn't true. I didn't try to kiss the bride. I wished I had never gone to the wedding. I wished I had been invisible when I danced with the bride.

It is time for a showdown, I told myself as I knocked on A & V's door. The bride and groom had been in town for two days, staying at A & V's house, and they were leaving in the evening.

She has grown older, I thought, while looking at the bride sitting on the sofa facing me while holding her two-month-old baby boy. I was ready to confront her. I wanted to yell, 'I didn't try to kiss you.' I wanted to tell her my truth. I looked at A & V who were with the groom in the kitchen preparing chicken legs, meat cutlets, and vegetables for the barbecue, then at the wine glass in my hand; a drunken truth, I told myself.

At the end of the evening, as we sat in the garden, the bride spoke of how she missed our city and began to recount her memories of it. When she uttered the word 'wedding', I wanted to cry out, no! Don't mention the kiss! And she didn't. But A looked at me and our eyes met. At that moment, I realized that A had never believed me and neither had anyone else.

I looked at the bride and the groom, who were sitting next to each other. I imagined them standing together. I imagined myself between their bodies. I imagined my head between their heads. I closed my eyes and I didn't want to imagine anymore.

Later that evening, I was talking alone with V when a sudden flash of A's gaze came back to me. All of a sudden, I said, 'Ok! Ok, I believe it. I believe that I kissed the bride.'

'You didn't kiss her,' V said. 'You tried to kiss her.'

'Ok! I believe I tried to kiss her. I believe it.'

The next day, despite my hangover, I was cheerful. I was relieved by the acceptance that I had tried to kiss the bride on her wedding night. I also decided to end our friendship without telling the bride and vowed never to write to her. I vowed never to talk about her or mention her name to anybody who knew her. In doing so, I hoped for a clean break of sorts from the whole affair, and if the memory of the attempted kiss were to return again, perhaps it would be milder or in any case less agonising.

Months later, V told me he'd soon visit the former bride.

Oh, I said to myself. I felt a sudden sense of humiliation. The attempted kiss returned to the forefront of my mind. I closed my eyes in resignation. I became sad, then disappointed with myself. I had thought my acceptance of the attempted kiss had healed me, but it hadn't. I felt hurt for reasons I wasn't even sure of. The bride, I thought, must have misunderstood the tilt of my head. After all, when I am slightly tipsy I usually dance by swaying my upper body; I move my shoulders up and down at the same time or one after another, and lean my head backwards and forwards or side to side. When I made my move, the violet and blue lights on the dance floor were sweeping over the bride's radiant white wedding dress. The dress was tight and fell to her knees, clinging to her thin frame and flat belly. As I stood between her and the groom, the bride with her dark curly short hair was smiling, displaying her fine white teeth beneath her dark red lips. She was moving her head side to side. *Did she get confused by the swaying of my head?* I asked myself. My face would have been close to hers, perhaps inches apart, and the groom's face must have been inches apart from the back of my head. Perhaps, when I was dancing between them, I was moving my head backwards and forwards.

For a long time, I experienced self-pity, remorse, regret, anguish and shame. How I am supposed to live with this? I kept asking myself. So I wrote this story.

THE GIRL AND THE CLOUD

The lowland was dry and barren, cut by a long stretch of dusty road. By the roadside, a young girl was lying on the ground face down, her head resting on her right cheek and both hands next to her head. The girl's lips were dry and her face was covered in dust. She was barefoot and wearing a dark yellow long-sleeved blouse with a dark grey floor-length skirt. Her face was wrapped in a grey headscarf decorated with black abstract patterns.

From time to time, the girl opened her eyes wide and tried hard not to close them, as if trying to stop herself from sleeping. And at times she lifted her head up slowly and stared at the horizon.

On the horizon there was an outline of hazy blue mountains. Below the mountains and against a desert mirage, several rows of white shapes resembling clouds or birds could be seen moving slowly and horizontally, rhythmically chanting:

Chaka... chaka... chaka... chakakaka
Chaka... chaka... chaka... chakakaka
Chaka... chaka... chaka... chakakaka
Chaka... chaka... chaka... chakakaka
Chaka... chaka... chaka.... chakakaka

The girl, using both hands for support, pulled her upper body up from the ground and turned to look over her shoulder.

The chants faded.

Some distance away, the girl saw a lorry in front of a desert mirage. She stared at the lorry for a while and tried to adjust herself to a sitting position, but fell back down and passed out.

The girl was asleep under the lorry. The lorry was burnt out. Around its charred remains, the debris of household furniture was scattered.

After an hour or two of sleep, the girl woke up. She put on a pair of sandals and got out from under the lorry.

The girl heard loud chants:

Chaka... chaka... chaka... chakakaka
Chaka... chaka... chaka... chakakaka
Chaka... chaka... chaka... chakakaka
Chaka... chaka... chaka... chakakaka
Chaka... chaka... chaka.... chakakaka

She stretched her arms with a yawn and wiped off the sand from her face. She looked around: emptiness.

The girl went back to the lorry. She pulled out a half-full dirty white transparent jerry can of water from under it. She took a sip and washed her face with a little water then dried it using part of her headscarf.

The chants continued:

Chaka... chaka... chaka... chakakaka
Chaka... chaka... chaka... chakakaka
Chaka... chaka... chaka... chakakaka
Chaka... chaka... chaka... chakakaka
Chaka... chaka... chaka.... chakakaka

The girl looked around and tilted her head back to look up at the sky; the sky was clear blue but for a small cumulus cloud.

The chants continued:

Chaka... chaka... chakakaka.
Chaka... chaka... chakakaka.
Chaka... chak...

'Stop it!' shouted the girl.

The chants stopped immediately. The girl looked around, then heard a voice speaking to her.

'Are you alone?'

The girl looked around again.

'Look up here. I am the one who is talking,' said the cloud.

The girl looked up in shock, stared at the cloud a while, and said, 'Do clouds talk?'

'Of course,' answered the cloud.

'That is impossible.'

'Nothing is impossible in life.'

'But—'

'Are you alone?' interrupted the cloud.

'Yes, I am alone,' said the girl. Looking at the sky, she added, 'You are alone too. Why?'

'I got lost,' answered the cloud.

'Lost!'

'Yes.'

The girl laughed.

'Who are you?' asked the cloud.

The girl ignored the cloud's question.

'Why are you here?' continued the cloud.

'Just wandering,' said the girl.

'Around here! There is nothing to see. It is awful,' said the cloud and laughed out loud.

'I don't care! It is my country,' shouted the girl, waving a clenched fist at the cloud.

'Ok! Ok! Calm down,' said the cloud.

The girl took out a small hand mirror from under the lorry. While looking at her reflection, she asked, 'Which way are you going?'

'I don't know yet,' answered the cloud.

'When will you know?'

'I don't know.'

The girl picked out an eyeliner pencil from her pocket and began to line her eyes. 'Ok, I am leaving now,' she said.

'See you, then,' answered the cloud.

The girl finished making up her eyes and looked at her face in the mirror. She waved goodbye to the cloud and, carrying the jerry can with one hand and the mirror with the other, walked away.

A few minutes later, the girl came back, walking lazily. She put the jerry can and the mirror on the ground and rested her back against one of the lorry's charred wheels.

'So you are back then,' said the cloud.

'Yes, I am just a bit tired,' said the girl.

Soft winds started to blow. The girl looked up and saw the cloud drifting away. She got up holding her jerry can and mirror and, running after the cloud, shouted, 'Which way are you going?'

'The way we are both going...for now,' answered the cloud.

The girl followed the cloud.

'Where do you come from?' asked the cloud.

'From the other side of the river,' answered the girl.

'I don't see any river around here. You must have walked a long way.'

'Yes.'

'So where exactly on the other side of the river?'

The girl didn't reply.

'Where are you going?' asked the cloud.

'I don't know,' answered the girl. 'You seem to be free. I wish I was you.'

'You can be a cloud if you like,' said the cloud.

'How?'

'If you lie on top of me, you will become a cloud.'

'Really?' The girl thought about it at length. 'No, I don't think I want to become a cloud.'

'Ok, we will become the cloud and the lonely girl.'

'I am not lonely,' shouted the girl. 'What about the lonely cloud and the girl?' she added after a pause.

'That doesn't ring very well—'

'The girl and the lonely cloud,' interrupted the girl.

'But—' said the cloud

'The girl and the cloud,' shouted the girl.

'That's it,' said the cloud. 'But there is a little problem. How can we get you up here?'

'Come down.'

'No, not now... Maybe later.'

After a long journey, they approached a steep hill. The girl stopped and rubbed the pouring sweat off her face while the cloud passed over the hill. The girl reluctantly followed the cloud and walked up and down a chain of steep hills. All of a sudden, the cloud stopped directly above a high hill's summit, closer to the girl's head.

The girl sat down and rested.

The sun disappeared behind the cloud. The cloud's shadow fell over the girl; she closed her eyes.

After the cloud's shadow passed by, the girl leapt to her feet and jumped up repeatedly in an attempt to touch the cloud, but it was in vain.

'Say something very loudly down into the valley,' said the cloud.

'Why?' asked the girl.

'Just say something very loudly,' said the cloud.

'Anything?'

'Yes, anything!'

'Hello!' the girl shouted.

'Hello... Hello... Hello,' came the echo.

'Hello,' shouted the girl again.

'Hello... Hello... Hello.'

'I met a wonderful cloud.'

'Wonderful cloud... Wonderful cloud... Wonderful cloud.'

'Ha-ha,' the cloud laughed out loud.

'Ha-ha... Ha-ha... Ha-ha.'

Later in the afternoon, the cloud set off again. The girl ran down the hill and followed the cloud through a narrow pass.

'Do you think they can keep a secret?' whispered the girl.

'Who?' asked the cloud.

'The ones who were talking back at us.'

'No one was talking to us, it was an echo!'

'Echo! What is that?'

'Echo is...Well... You should know,' said the cloud. 'You said this is your country. Now, leave me alone... You talk too much.'

'But... but I just want to be your friend,' protested the girl.

'You really want to be my friend?' asked the cloud.

'Yes, of course.'

'We are friends then.'

'Thank you. I wish I could hug you.'

'You will. Nothing is impossible in life.' After a short pause, the cloud said, 'No, we shouldn't be friends.'

'Why not?'

'Because we may hate each other tomorrow.'

'That is a cruel thing to say,' said the girl.

'Ok! Ok! I am your friend, but I only love my family,' said the cloud.

'Do you have a family?' asked the girl.

'Of course! Do you think you are the only one who has a family?' the cloud answered, 'We were a happy cloud family. I loved father and mother. My sister loved father so much but my mother loved my brother even more. I loved my sister and brother...' 'Where are they now?' interrupted the girl.

'After the wind struck hard, my father began to wander round and round in circles until he disappeared. My mother and brother went away in a straight line to the west, and my sister to the northeast... Anyway, it is too much. I don't want to remember. Please don't ask me about my family again.'

They continued in silence.

Night came. The moon and stars shone.

The cloud stopped. The girl sat on the ground, took a sip from her jerry can, and asked, 'Are we going to spend the night here?'

'I don't know,' answered the cloud.

'Tell me a story.'

'What story?'

'Any story.' The girl thought for a while and said, 'What about a story from one hundred and one nights?'

'I have never heard of one hundred and one nights,' said the cloud. 'Do you mean one thousand and one nights?'

'Is that so?' wondered the girl.

'Oh dear, you must have read a censored version,' said the cloud, laughing. 'You missed nine hundred nights.'

'Then there are many stories you can tell me,' said the girl.

'Of course! And they are wonderful stories.'

'Let's start then.'

'Are you a slave?'

'No. Why do you ask?'

'All the black people in the stories are slaves. I was wondering which slave story—'

'Will you just tell me a story before I sleep?' interrupted the girl, lying down on her back.

'All right, the story... The story of Baraka and the coloured fish. The fisherman and the genie went to a lake. The genie ordered the fisherman to throw his net into the lake... Is that right?... Yes, the fisherman caught four fish, each one in a different colour, one white, another red, another blue, the other yellow... Is that right?... Yes, the fish spoke in classical Arabic... The fish spoke... Can you believe it? Oh! I've forgotten. But let me tell you another story. The story of the three apples. One morning, a man went for a walk in a garden... Is that it?... Yes, he found three apples... And... Oh! Who needs to hear about apples... Never mind, I remember this one... The story of Bakhit the slave, who used to tell his masters exactly one lie every year, so that they fell out with one another... I think he used to get sold every time... Oh! I've forgotten it...'

The moon disappeared behind the cloud, its shadow slowly drifted over the girl. The cloud noticed the girl was asleep and recited:

'Your image I see before me whether near or far
And your name inhabits my tongue...'

The cloud then whistled a while, and said, 'Sleep my dear... Sleep my dear little... If only I knew your name.'

In the morning, the orange sun slid up the horizon,

The cloud chanted:

Chaka... chaka... chakakaka.
Chaka... chaka... chakakaka.
Chaka... chaka... chakakaka.
Chaka... chaka... chakakaka.

The girl woke up, and shouted, 'Will you stop it? It is annoying!'

'What is annoying you?' asked the cloud.

'That song of yours.'

'I am not singing. I am meditating.'

'Where did you learn it anyway?'

'I was somewhere recently. I don't remember where... I saw a group of around thirty people. They were lined up in five or six rows and were all wearing white clothes, with white turbans on their heads. They were chanting or perhaps meditating, all in one voice. I liked the idea of meditation,' said the cloud said. 'The only thing I remember now is; chaka chakakaka... chaka chaka chakakaka... chaka chakakaka... chaka chaka chakakaka...'

'Ok! Ok! I've heard enough,' shouted the girl.

'By the way, my dear... May I ask what is your name?'

The girl ignored the cloud and sat up. She looked at her jerry can; there was very little water left. She had a sip.

'Ok, so you don't know where you come from,' said the cloud. 'Who are you? Where are you going? You don't want to tell me your name, and yet you want to be my friend... hmm!'

'We are friends!' shouted the girl.

'Oh, dear, oh, dear!'

'Ok, my name is Fatima.'

'Fatima! That is a really nice name.'

'Thank you.'

'Fatima, tell me, what do you want from me?'

'Want from you?'

'You only want to be my friend because you want something from me.'

'I don't want anything from you. Only to be your friend.'

'Are you sure?'

'Of course.'

'We are friends then.'

Later on, Fatima looked at her jerry can and asked, 'Can you see a river?'

'I think I can see a lake surrounded by green trees...' said the cloud.

Fatima drank most of the water from her can and washed her face with what was left. She looked at her face in the mirror, reapplied her eyeliner and lay on her back.

'Fatima, you are really pretty,' said the cloud.

'Thank you,' answered Fatima with a smile.

A moment of silence followed.

'Fatima, do you want to be my girlfriend?' asked the cloud.

'What?' exclaimed Fatima.

'Be my girlfriend!'

'Be your girlfriend? Are you mad?'

'No, I am not mad!'

'For a start, I can't have a boyfriend. I can only have a husband,' said Fatima.

'Marry me then,' said the cloud.

'Marry you?'

'I am in love with you. Marry me, please.'

'I can't. How can I marry a cloud? I want to marry a person; a handsome boy of my age. Don't get me wrong, I like you and you are a very beautiful cloud...'

'But you love handsome boys and not beautiful clouds.'

'Yes. No, no... I like you a lot. You are a true friend.'

'What is the point of being a true friend to a pretty girl like you?'

'Anyway, you don't want to come down here and I can't get up there, so what is the point of us getting married?'

'We can find a solution.'

'A solution! That's impossible.'

'Nothing is impossible in life.'

'This is impossible!'

'Just say yes.'

'Oh, god! This is impossible... Impossible! You are a crazy cloud!'

Suddenly, a gust of wind blew. The cloud moved away swiftly. Fatima got up, picked up her jerry can and mirror, and ran after the cloud, screaming, 'Wait! Wait!'

After a while, the cloud slowed down and then suddenly stopped. Fatima caught the cloud. She sat down, breathless, and asked, 'Why did you do that?'

The cloud didn't reply.

Fatima shook her head in disbelief.

Suddenly, a jet flew above them. Fatima put the jerry can on the ground and lay face down on the ground, arms and legs spread. After sensing the danger had passed, she picked up the can and ran after the cloud.

'Why were you lying like that?' asked the cloud.

'I was told if I saw a fighter jet I had to lie like that,' answered Fatima.

'But why like that?'

'I don't know.'

In the evening, the cloud stopped above a tree. Fatima sat under the tree and asked, 'How far are we from the lake?'

'I don't know,' answered the cloud.

'You don't know! I have run out of water. We have to find the lake,' said Fatima.

Night came, bringing with it the moon and stars.

The thirst was unbearable to Fatima. She sat on her jerry can and peed in it. She smelled it and turned away, disgusted. After hesitating for a moment, Fatima drank a sip and immediately threw up what she had drunk.

'Are you all right, Fatima?' asked the cloud.

'I am fine,' answered Fatima.

Fatima leant her back against a tree trunk, and asked, 'Do you know the city behind the blue mountains?'

'Of course,' said the cloud. 'Are you going there?'

'No.'

'What do you want to know about it?'

'Tell me about the blue mountains.'

'The mountains are blue. They are magnificent and breathtaking.'

'And the city?'

'It is behind the mountains. It is a big city with lots of palm trees lining the streets.'

'And the people?'

'So young, so handsome, so generous.'

'And the food?'

'Delicious foul mudammas with garlic and herbs, topped with sesame oil, falafel, salad and white cheese or egg.'

'Do they have meat?'

'Yes, of course! Delicious fried lamb and chicken stew.'

'What do they drink?'

'Fruit juices! Oh, and they have an ice-cream shop...'

'Oh! An ice-cream shop!'

Fatima lay on her back and gazed at the cloud through the tree leaves, then she closed her eyes dreamily and slept.

In the morning, the sun rose.

The cloud chanted:

Chaka... chaka... chakakaka
Chaka... chaka... chakakaka
Chaka... chaka... chakakaka
Chaka... chaka... chakakaka
Chaka... chaka... chakakaka

Fatima woke up. She sat and looked at her jerry can; there was little of her pee left. Fatima screwed her eyes shut and drank the pee.

The sun rose in the sky. Fatima, looking very tired and very thirsty, pleaded, 'Please, please... let's go to the lake.'

The cloud made Fatima waited for a long time before moving.

'So you love handsome boys, not beautiful ones,' said the cloud.

'Yes,' Fatima answered.

'Do you know why you don't like beautiful boys?'

'They aren't my type.'

'No! You just don't want a rival for your mirror.'

'Shut up! Just shut up! I don't want to talk to you anymore,' Fatima yelled.

In the evening they approached a burned lorry. Fatima couldn't believe her eyes, and said, 'We are back at the same place where I met you two days ago.'

'Are we?'

'Yes! I think we have been going round in circles.'

'It might be another burnt lorry.'

Fatima was convinced that it was the same lorry. She shook her head in disbelief and sat on the ground, burying her face in her hands.

Then came another night, and with it the moon and stars.

Fatima rested on her side and stared at the dark line of the horizon. She shed a few tears and wiped them away with her finger, tasting them. She felt the warmth of the liquid in her mouth. Fatima looked up at the cloud. Suddenly, her face lit up. She gathered all her strength, sat up and asked, 'What do you think about when you are thirsty?'

'Watermelon,' answered the cloud.

Fatima laughed out loud, but the cloud did not. 'Do clouds laugh?' Fatima asked.

'Of course,' replied the cloud. 'You have heard me laugh a few times.'

'I don't remember. Let me hear you laugh.'

The cloud laughed out loud a few times. Fatima laughed with him.

Moments passed in silence.

'Do clouds cry?'

'Yes, I mean no,' said the cloud, 'No, we don't cry, hardly at all'

A long time passed in silence.

'Why are you quiet, Fatima?' asked the cloud.

'Nothing. It is nothing,' answered Fatima. She turned her head towards the lorry, and said, 'You see this lorry?'

'Yes.'

'It was bombed by a fighter jet.'

'Really?'

'Yes. I was a passenger.'

'What?'

'I asked the driver to stop to go for a pee. I left the lorry alone with my jerry can and my mirror. As I was coming back, the fighter jet bombed the lorry. Nobody survived.'

'Who was in there?'

'People from my home town... There were many families with their children at the back of the lorry sitting on their luggage.'

There was a moment of silence.

'We had all just survived a massacre in my home town,' Fatima said.

'How many people died?'

'How do I know? I ran away.'

'When was it?'

'A few days ago.'

'No, no,' said the cloud, after a moment. 'You don't look like you have been in a massacre.'

'How do you want me to look?' Fatima enquired.

'I don't know. I have never seen you distraught or crying.'

Fatima suddenly began to cry. Her sobs became louder and louder. After a while the cloud shouted, 'Enough! Stop it, please.'

Fatima carried on crying.

'Ok! Ok! I believe you. I believe that you have survived a massacre and you are lucky,' said the cloud.

'Lucky!' scoffed Fatima.

'Yes, lucky to be here.'

Fatima buried her head in her hands and shook it in disbelief.

'With all due respect, what evidence do you have?' asked the cloud.

'Don't you believe what I say?' said Fatima.

'It isn't that. It is just that anybody can say or invent anything.'

'What about this lorry?'

'You could have been a passer-by'

'I swear to God I was a passenger,' Fatima shouted. 'I swear to God I was sitting in the front seat. The driver asked me to sit next to him. I swear to God I went for a pee. I swear to G—'

'Swearing doesn't prove anything,' interrupted the cloud.

'How can I make you believe me?' asked Fatima.

'Words are not enough.'

Fatima thought for a moment, and said, 'I have a gun wound in my…' and pointed to her bum.

'Can I see it?' asked the cloud.

'See what?'

'Your wound.'

'No! No way!' cried out Fatima.

Night set in. Fatima cried for a while, then dried her tears with both hands, and said, 'It was in the late evening. I was looking for my cat when the soldiers burst into our yard. I hid on the rooftop of our house and saw everything.'

'What did you see?' asked the cloud.

'My brother was first to come out of the house. They caught him and tied his hands and feet together with his arms wrapped around his legs. They then put a stick under his knees and started calling him number eight.'

'Why number eight?'

'I don't know. I suppose they'd forced his body into a number eight shape,' Fatima said. 'Then my father came out of the house; they shot him dead. And then my mother came out with my two-year old baby sister. They shot my mother dead. They picked up my baby sister and smashed her against the wall. My older sister entered the yard, holding a lantern. They grabbed her and dragged her around the yard. The lantern fell to the ground. Our donkey began to bray and started running like crazy. They got hold of the donkey and poured petrol over her and then threw the lantern at her. The yard lit up. The donkey brayed loudly, jumping up and down. Then they raped my sister and shot her dead. Then they beat up my brother and shot him in the head.'

'Still looking like number eight?'

'Yes. When they left I cried for hours. The next day I got out of the house and saw so many people dead in the street. They smelled so bad...'

'I am really sorry to hear that,' said the cloud.

'Sorry! Is that all you can say?'

'What do you want me to say?'

'Nothing. Just cry.'

'I am afraid I cannot do that,' said the cloud.

Fatima fell to the ground, fists and face clenched in anger.

Time passed.

Fatima was lying on the ground face down.

'How old are you?' asked the cloud.

Fatima didn't reply.

'How old are you, Fatima?' asked the cloud again.

Fatima was asleep.

In the morning, Fatima was still asleep directly under the cloud, curled up and hugging her jerry can.

The cloud chanted:

Chaka... chaka... chakakaka
Chaka... chaka... chakakaka
Chaka... chaka... chakakaka
Chaka... chaka... chakakaka
Chaka... chaka... chakakaka
Chaka... chaka... chakakaka
Chaka... chaka... chakakaka

Fatima woke and asked, 'What time is it?'

'What time? How should I know?' said the cloud. 'Let's say it is another morning.'

Fatima looked at her face in the mirror. Her face was covered in dust and her mouth was dry. She wiped off as much dust as she could from her face, put down her mirror and stared at the cloud without blinking for a while.

The cloud didn't say anything.

Fatima got up, picked up a small piece of debris and tiredly threw it at the cloud. But the cloud was beyond her reach. She threw two more pieces without touching the cloud. Fatima gave up and sat on the ground. 'Have I ever seen a cloud with no emotions?' she shouted, pointing her finger at the cloud. 'Yes, it's you!'

The cloud said nothing.

'And I was a fool to believe in you,' said Fatima, 'and to say that I wanted to be free as a cloud—'

'I am free! Everyone dreams to be free as a cloud,' said the cloud.

'You only go one way. Round and round... I hate you. You should be sent to prison.'

'I am free! Unlike you, I float... You walk...' shouted the cloud.

'Marry me please... Marry me please,' Fatima mimicked the cloud. 'You don't even have a cock, and you want to make love to me!'

Fatima looked at the cloud; her face was full of hatred. She slowly fell to her knees, then collapsed on the ground, unconscious.

The sun disappeared behind the cloud. The cloud looked dark and cast his shadow over Fatima's motionless body; Fatima woke up. She looked up at the cloud and then at the jerry can. Fatima crawled slowly towards the can. She grabbed it and turned on her back. Holding the can with both hands, she held it to her open mouth and shook it up and down. But there was no pee left.

'Do you want to make a deal?' the cloud asked.

'What kind of deal?' asked Fatima, throwing away the can.

'Well,' said the cloud said. 'I could give you three drops of water if you would tell me your real name.'

'I told you my name is Fatima.'

'No, it isn't.'

'All right, it is Rahwa.'

'I don't believe you.'

'I swear to God it's Rahwa.'

'I don't believe you,' the cloud said. 'I will call you Girl.'

'All right!' shouted the girl. 'Call me what you want. Just give me some drops of water.'

'Ok! Ok! Are you ready for those drops?'

The girl opened her mouth wide.

Three drops fell in quick succession on the girl's forehead.

'Sorry, I missed,' said the cloud.

The girl was unimpressed. But as she was about to shout, the cloud said, 'I'll give you five more drops if you take your shoes off.'

The girl immediately took off her shoes. This time, the drops fell into the girl's mouth.

'If you take off your headscarf, I'll give you ten drops,' said the cloud.

'No way!'

Silence ensued. Then the girl, in tears, took her headscarf off and put it around her neck.

'You have beautiful hair,' said the cloud.

The girl didn't say anything.

'Throw your scarf away,' said the cloud.

The girl reluctantly did so and opened her mouth. Ten drops fell into it.

'I'll give you thirty drops if you take your blouse off,' said the cloud.

'No! No! Please no,' cried out the girl.

The cloud didn't say anything.

After a long hesitation, the girl took off her blouse and sat covering her chest with the fabric; she had no bra.

'Throw it away,' said the cloud.

The girl threw away her blouse. Thirty drops fell into her mouth. The girl licked her lips and then covered her breasts with both hands.

'If you take your dress off, I'll give you fifty drops,' said the cloud.

The girl took off her dress. The cloud gave her fifty drops.

'If you take your knickers off I'll give you one hundred drops,' said the cloud.

'I thought you were different,' said the girl.

'From who?' enquired the cloud.

'People.'

'From the ones who massacred your town or the handsome ones?'

'So, you believe my stories.'

'Turn around.'

'Turn around?'

'Show me your bum. I want see your gun wound.'

The girl pointed to her bum, and said 'It is here. I won't show it to you.'

'You see... you are lying. You lied to me twice already!'

'Ok, ok! I lied to you about the gun wound and my name...'

'And the massacre?'

'I lied to you about the dates. The massacre happened a year ago.'

The cloud didn't say anything.

'I swear to God everything else I've told you is true,' said the girl.

The cloud didn't say anything.

Under the afternoon sun, the girl was clinging to her jerry can; her entire naked body was covered in sweat and dust.

Time passed.

The girl, with a weak voice, pleaded, 'If you do not cry, I will die.'

'And if I do so will I,' answered the cloud.

Time passed.

The sun disappeared.

In the morning, the cloud chanted:

Chaka... chaka... chakakaka
Chaka... chaka... chakakaka
Chaka... chaka... chakakaka
Chaka... chaka... chakakaka
Chaka... chaka... chakakaka
Chaka... chaka... chakakaka
Chaka... chaka... chakakaka
Chaka... chaka... chakakaka
Chaka... chaka... chakakaka

The girl was lying on the ground on her back, under the cloud. Her eyes were wide open. She couldn't close them.

The cloud cried.

THE FILM SHOP

I

Two lovers, a prince and a princess, sit on a carpet. The carpet floats on a small lake. A tree sliced in half. A village. A donkey drags a cart. Pots.

Those were some of the images that stayed with me from a Japanese film that I once saw late at night either on BBC2 or Channel 4. I was stoned. In those days, I didn't have a VHS player, so I used to get stoned and wait till after 12 am for foreign films to be shown on television because they were subtitled. Years later, when I was scanning the shelves of The Film Shop on Liverpool Road, I instantly recognised the cover image: Mizoguchi's *Ugetsu Monogatari or Tales of Moonlight and Rain*. But the two lovers weren't a prince and a princess but a poor villager and a ghost. They weren't floating but reclining in ecstasy on a blanket laid over a patch of grass. The tree wasn't sliced but two trees, standing next to each other. The cart wasn't dragged by a donkey but by a man with his brother pushing it at the back.

I was sad when Gabrielle told me that The Film Shop would close down. At that time, I was hardly renting any films as I was busy writing a film script. The film shop used to open at 4 pm and normally got busy after 5 pm, so I had an hour or so to talk to Gabrielle; she behind the desk and I in front of her. Gabrielle used to read my film scripts, and I hers. We'd spend the hour exchanging ideas and opinions. Gabrielle was a filmmaker and was born in the hometown of Jane Eyre's author. I rented and watched a film adaptation of the book, and saw the surprise in Gabrielle's eyes when I told her that I never read the Brontë sisters.

I asked myself why I hadn't joined a long time ago. I'd often passed by. But it wasn't until I was told I'd be made redundant from my job as a photographic technician that I went inside. I walked aimlessly through the streets of Islington the day after that news, and stopped by the window of The Film Shop. For a £10 monthly fee I could rent up to 3 films a day. Why not? I'd have time. I glanced at the Barnsbury job centre on my way home thinking that I'd be back there in a month's time. Each day for the next four weeks, I worked at Photofusion in Brixton, then late in the evenings when most of the staff had left, printed hundreds of pages of articles about world cinema directors to take home and read.

Almost every day unemployed I sat in a café in Goswell Street. The cafe owner would change the name of the cafe from time to time; it was café @ or Fuck Coffee or Fuck me Coffee or Goswell Road Coffee. Whatever its name was, I was there on the mornings from around seven (sometimes in the winter from around six-thirty so I could experience the darkness morphing into light) and in the afternoons from around four. Though in the winter I'd go as early as three because of the early sunset.

I sat at a favourite spot opposite a large window and did nothing for an hour or two. I talked to no one and no one talked to me. My brain recalled films I'd seen or dreamed up films I wanted to make. My eyes observed the passers-by. And sometimes my brain, eyes, and heart would collaborate and concentrate on *a whole duration*: I'd look without any interruption from the moment when someone or something enters the window frame until he, she or it leaves it, be it any living being or even a leaf at the mercy of the winds. I once saw a child tie a red balloon to a street litter bin and leave the frame. The balloon was dancing on the air. I watched the balloon for more than half hour and I was expecting it to fly away at any moment until *she* entered the frame and punctured the balloon with her cigarette butt. I saw her, I believe, more than eleven *whole durations* on days after that. In each duration, I had different emotions. She would enter from the left side of the window, with her bobbed haircut, and always smoking. The second time I saw her was from her back for almost the whole duration. And there was this duration where she was talking on her mobile phone and smoking while looking directly at me or at her nails, that may have been freshly airsprayed at the Chinese nail salon nearby. Then she disappeared for a while. But I saw her coming out of a phone box, holding call cards. I felt as if I saw someone famous. The lady in so many silent frames. I almost waved my hands at her, and wanted to shout, 'Hi!' But before I could do that, she stood facing me. She looked at me coldly. She then gave me one of the call cards and walked away. I looked at the picture on the card, it wasn't her, and there was a name on the card: Nananana. I really wanted to ask her if they'd give any discounts for someone as unemployed like me. But she instantly disappeared from my view. I saw her for the final time, when she entered the frame, wearing a black boucle coat. And then as she was trying to cross the street, she was run over by a pizza delivery boy on a motorbike. I don't know if she lived or died but I didn't leave my seat.

Gabrielle complained about spiralling rent costs, Pirate Bay and Bit Torrent, LoveFilm, Netflix and Apple releasing its macs without DVD players. However, she also told me that the owner – who once recommended me *The Third Part of the Night*, a Polish film that I too would recommend to anyone, but I wouldn't want to see again – was willing to sell if he could find a buyer.

When it comes to sound, I am man+machine. And this fusion with the machine reproduces, badly, the sounds from TV, Radio or phone. And it is even worse with an immediate human natural speech, where neither I, my doctor, my audiologist or friends will know when or what I will hear, if it isn't a one to one situation in a quiet room. That is why when I am watching films I rely entirely on subtitles, including for English language films. So, I see and read films at the same time (I normally have to sacrifice one or the other). The average speed of human speech is around 180 words per mins, but with Orson Welles's films, I suspect, the average speed exceeds double that. People talking fast all the time, and a voice-over decorates every frame, and the camera pans and moves too. And I have to watch his images for 2 hours at 360 words a minute.

Gabrielle told me that a film producer, an Islingtonian, was willing to buy The Film Shop provided he gets a concrete idea for revamping the shop. I told Gabrielle about what Godard said of American cinema (almost all of Godard's one liners have now became a cliché): that Hollywood only makes one film a year. So, I asked her to tell the owner about my idea to replace the American section (aside from the classics) and triple their collection of world cinema, find and add out of print DVDs. The next day, Gabrielle told me the would-be owner said 'no.' I then proposed to reinvent The Film Shop as a Film and Theatre Café. And again, replacing the American section (aside from the classics) with theatre DVDs. There were a few theatres nearby such as Almeida Theatre, King's Head Theatre Pub and Old Red Lion Theatre Pub, and perhaps they could attract more customers from those spaces. The would-be owner's answer, through Gabrielle, was 'no'. As the deadline for its closure loomed, I pleaded with Gabrielle to tell this faceless would-be owner that I was prepared to design a leaflet appeal to save the shop (I had already designed a DVD cover for one of Gabrielle's award winning short films), and that I would distribute this leaflet myself to every house in Islington. I knew I could do this because I once worked as Pizza leaflet ad distributor. I knew every single street in Islington. The operation would be easy for me, and all of this free of charge. But again, the answer was 'no'.

Every day, I used to take different routes to go to The Film Shop and different ones to get back to my flat in Kings Cross. The only streets I avoided were the streets that lead to the Jobcentre. Sometimes I wondered if I was hallucinating. There was such contrast between my silent room and the roar in the nearby streets. My moods would swing from low to high. If I saw the Islingtonians in the streets, our eyes would meet but to only for them to veer off and look the other way. Or I'd look down at the pavement or through the Islingtonians' windows, at the ground floor or basement; the kitchens or living rooms. And there were those occasions when I'd walk at dawn. The streets would be empty, and I'd even notice the lamp posts being switched off. On one late morning, when I was in a low mood, I stood next to a Flight Centre branch in Upper Street. My right foot was resting on the wall behind me. I was staring at the sky, waiting for the partial eclipse of the sun. All of a sudden, I saw three Italian women, seemingly in high spirits, walk past me and into an office. I guessed that they were Italian because of the way they gesticulated as they spoke. One was blonde and the other two were brunettes. They were dressed in Eritrean traditional dress (white woven cotton clothing) and had their hair braided in traditional Eritrean style (in London, I have seen western women dressed in west African dress, Chinese, Indian or Tibetan dresses but I'd never seen one wearing an Eritrean dress). But then the blonde one, who had a sad look in her eyes when she stopped conversing with her friends, stood outside the door and looked up at the sky and then at the door or perhaps at me. I thought I saw her lips moving, and I said, 'Are you talking to me?' I watched her moving past me as if I were a statue and through the open door.

The Film Shop closed down when I was set to embark on a study of silent cinema. The idea of the study came to me when suddenly the battery of my hearing aid ran out while I was in the cafe. I kept my hearing aid on but heard only muffled sound from the outside world and the constant low buzzes and hums from inside. It was a Sunday afternoon. There was a DJ playing Drum and Bass music, which turned to nothing but a low thud. I was sitting on a two-seat sofa. An old man sat at the sofa opposite me. He was holding a glass of white wine, his hand shaking. He put the glass down to close to the edge of the table. I looked at it for a few seconds, but I couldn't warn him because I don't like to speak when I cannot hear my own voice. The glass fell to the floor. The old man didn't move at all. An elderly waitress came and picked up 5 large fragments of the broken glass one at a time, and put them on the dustpan. Holding a sponge with her left hand, she wiped the floor. I tried to count the number of the wipes she did, but to no avail. Using the sponge, the waitress picked up the remaining small fragments of the glass and put them onto the dustpan. She got up and walked away.

One afternoon, I was at the café reading a DVD supplement of *Humanity and Paper Balloons*. In the supplement, it said that its director Sadao Yamanaka - a close friend of Tokyo Story director Ozo – was visited by Kurosawa when he was still an assistant director during the shoot of the film.

The Seven Samurai director remembered that even though the weather was perfectly fine, everybody was just standing around idly, peering up at the sky. He learnt they were waiting for a cloud to waft over a warehouse on the set...

Just then I saw a woman with a Great Dane sitting opposite me on the sofa. Garbo, I wanted to shout. She really looked like Greta Garbo. I had a cut-out picture of Garbo looking down, with her index finger on her forehead, after I read somewhere that she was the idea of beauty in Cinema. But my Garbo picture was in black and white and this woman's eyes were green with thick red painted lips. Could she be related to Garbo? Perhaps she was her great granddaughter. But Garbo never married or had any children, so perhaps, a great granddaughter of a cousin. The woman looked at the DVD cover on the table, and said, 'You like At..aus movs?' I lipread.

'What?' I said, breaking into uncomfortable speech.

The woman looked at me and then at my hearing aid, and said loudly, 'DO YOUUU LIKE AAAART HAAAAOOOS MOVIIIIES?'

'Yes,' I said.

'AMAAAZING... AMAZING!' the woman shouted again and kept nodding her head while looking at me. And then, she shouted, 'HAAVE YOU WAAATCHED ALII FEEEAR EEEEATS THA SOOOUL?'

'No,' I said. Now, I became convinced that she isn't related to Garbo because she had an English accent, and that because she had her dog with her, then she must be a local, an Islingtonian, perhaps.

'FAAASBINDAAAR. FAAASBINDAAAR,' the woman said.

'Not yet,' I said, 'But I know Fassbinder...'

'It is an AMAZING MOOOVIE. AAALI REMIINDS MEEEE OOOF YOU...' the woman shouted.

'Thank you. I will watch it.'

'YOU ARE AMAZING!'

'I want to be alone. I want to be left alone,' I said

I signed on every fortnight, on Tuesday mornings. I hated those mornings! It was on those mornings that I sunk low and felt useless. My depression would begin on Monday evenings. And it would go on until I was on my way to the Jobcentre, which was 15 mins walk from where I lived. And during those 15 minutes my worries would intensify wondering whether she, my job coach, would accept the list of job searches that I had conducted, applied for or would apply for. In truth, I hadn't searched or applied for any jobs at all. Instead, I took notes while I watched films. Once inside the Jobcentre, a large open plan office, I had to wait to be called in by my job coach. The time would pass too slowly, even if I had to wait just 5 minutes. In those times, I'd pretend to read a book. And the book would be very close to my face, almost covering it so that I was not seen. So that nobody could make eye contact. Trust me, when you are in a Jobcentre, you don't want to show your parasite-like face to either the staff or the others who have parasite-like faces like you. When I met my job coach in a small private and glass framed space, I'd recount, of course, my job-hunting news. I once told her that I rewrote my CV so that I could apply for a job as a black cab driver. After a brief pause, she said, 'It takes the average person between 2 to 4 years to learn the blue book'. She suggested looking instead for a job as a mini cab driver. But I replied that, due to my deafness, I would not be able to take job details over the radio or by phone. Then I went home knowing that I'd have 13 more days to watch films. Another time I told my job coach that I was looking for a job as a hairdresser. But then and suddenly, my job coach turned her face away from me. I saw her face sadden and tears cloud her eyes.

'I was a hairdresser,' she said, 'I had a salon. I met my late husband Antony there. He was one of my customers.' She paused, then carried on without looking at me, 'He committed suicide a few days after we got married. Not long after, I sold the salon, left my town and moved to London...'

'I am really sorry...' I said, staring at her beautiful, ageing face.

'Anyway,' she interrupted, 'You wouldn't be able to do this job. It involves a lot of listening to customers. You need to look at their hair rather than their face and you rely mostly on the lips to hear people…'

'What a shame!' I lied, 'I really wanted to meet new people and make friends.'

I walked a lot with Bef, around the streets of Islington. Bef worked in Islington Local History Centre as a Heritage Officer. Once, we walked around Barnsbury and I asked him to tell me something about it.

'The Barnsbury tdy…' Bef said.

'Wait, wait,' I interrupted Bef. I moved to his left side as my hearing aid is on my right ear, 'Go on.'

'Its nEt treets, well mantaned houses… Lanscape square, shops… Botiik, is…' Bef said

'Say that again,' I said.

'The streets are uncogisabl from the povety years foowing th Second Wod Waar,' Bef said.

'Can you tell me about the residents?' I asked.

'Leaf wing and labour suppotres…'

'Can you say that again,' I interrupted.

'Laber SUPPORTERS,' said Bef, 'They were acchticts, panners…'

'Wait! WAIT,' I interrupted, 'Let the truck pass.'

It was a large goods vehicle. We waited till the truck's noise receded. 'Where were we?' I asked.

'Those new residents fomed the Bansbury Assoshin…They saved old building from demotion…'

'Demoation?'

'DEMOLITION,'Bef shouted, 'I am tired of repeating.'

'Who lives in Bransbury?'

'Middle-class…Middle-class. Fashionable middle-class. Metropolitans class.'

'Where are the working class?'

'Shit out...'

'What?'

'SHIPPED out!'

'To where?'

Bef pointed towards Caledonian road, and said 'The tower boocks, in Caddonian road.'

'Were they happy to move out?' I asked

'I said,' Bef shouted, 'SHIPPED OUT!'

'I heard there are new gentry now days.' I said

'They are banks...' Bef said.

'Banks!'

'Bankers, BANKERS!

'What happened to the middle class?'

'Most ass been outpiced...'

'What? Out pissed... Spicid?'

'No! OUTPRICED. OUTPRICED! I am tired of shouting,' Bef shouted

Bef was one of the people who rarely complained about repeating words for me. Bef was born in Ethiopia, Addis Ababa. He arrived in London with his parents, aged five. Bef studied at SOAS, University of London, the history and geography of Africa. He joined The Foreign Legion when he couldn't find a job in London. But his career in the Legion ended in a court martial and he moved to Addington, south of Croydon. When Bef began working in Islington, he was still writing his memoires. I read part of them in which Bef recalls the heat of Djibouti and his beautiful young local girlfriend, Raheela. Bef was a chief of his section when he was discharged. A handsome young man joined the Legion and Bef grew jealous of him and his popularity. He sent the young man on an expedition without a compass and to his death in the harsh deserts of the Afar region, in the borders between Djibouti and Ethiopia.

At The Film Shop, Ritjana chose her favourite film - Pasolini's *Medea* - and I Tsai Ming Liang's *I Don't Want to Sleep Alone*. At home, I said to Ritjana, while trying to conceal my smile, 'Since I have seen *Medea* it would be better to watch,' I pointed at the DVD title, *I don't want to sleep alone,* 'You've watched Medea...,' Ritjana stared at me and then asked what the film was about. I thought for a while, and said, 'It is about the body and a double mattress. The suppressed emotions, desire and longings. ... And love'

While we were watching *I Don't Want to Sleep Alone*, I kept on looking at Ritjana through the corners of my eyes. On the one hand, I was hoping that she wouldn't get bored as words are rarely spoken in the film. And on the other, that she may get aroused; there are lots of sexual scenes without them being pornographic. Ritjana's eyes, during the entire film, were fixated on the screen. When the film finished, she exclaimed, 'Wow! Wow! What a film. This is my favourite film now!' Later on, we went to Kings Head Theatre Pub, in Upper Street. But we were thrown out after Ritjana drunkenly flashed her boobs at me while we were sitting on one of the theatre seats. The theatre was at the back of the bar and normally opened its doors for regulars after a play ended. As I was walking Ritjana to Caledonian road, so she could take the bus to go home to her husband, we stopped at Lonsdale Square. We kissed passionately and then I climbed the metal rails of the garden on impulse, hoping we could have a little privacy. But Ritjana couldn't jump; she had a prosthetic leg.

I once asked Gabrielle about the shop's main customers. 'Posh,' she said, loudly. I not only heard her say 'P' but the 'oosh'. I then asked her, 'What are they like?' 'POOSH,' she said, loudly again, shrugging her shoulder. 'What kind of films do they rent?' I asked. She pointed to the Hollywood commercial section on her right.

One late afternoon, I got out of my door on my way to the film shop. A few steps away, I was stopped by two policemen. One of the policemen stood, facing me directly. He looked at my right hand and said, 'What is that?

'Tobacco roller,' I said.

He looked at my eyes for a moment then suspiciously at my hand, and said,

'Smoke it. SMOKE IT!'

I took a long drag.

'Blow it out,' shouted the policeman, 'Blow IT OUT.'

I blew out. A thick cloud of smoke engulfed the policeman's face. The policeman closed his eyes for a while, seemingly restraining himself. Once the smoke cleared from around his face, the policeman opened his eyes, and said, 'You look stoned. Did you smoke at home? Your eyes look glazed.'

'No,' I said, 'I gave up hashish... I was watching this all day...' I showed him what I was holding in my left hand. They were Béla Tarr's Satantango DVDs.

Job seekers allowance was scarcely enough to pay for my bills and food. I couldn't go out apart from to a café, twice a day, to drink the cheapest coffee or tea. The only time I went out for a drink, was when a friend would invite me and pay for me. Most of the time, I went out with Bef. My financial situation was getting harder by the day. Once I was on a crowded train when I saw a man holding a broadsheet newspaper, folded in half, moving closer to a man in a suit. I watched closely. I saw him edge towards the man in the suit in the crowded carriage till their bellies touched each other. As the train was about to stop, the man with the paper folded the newspaper with his right hand and then with his left. I knew the man's wallet was inside. When the doors of the train opened, the man with the paper quickly left the train carriage. I bought a book titled: *The Prince of Pickpockets* by Richard S. Lambert. I read it day and night and practiced pickpocketing at home. I used a small notebook and drilled myself in picking it out with my index and middle finger from the inside pocket of my jacket. I also hung my jacket at the back of my room's door, put my wallet on my jacket's pocket and practiced picking it using a newspaper, like the pickpocket on the tube. I took the Victoria line from Oxford street. I stood in front of a man wearing a black suit. I looked at him while pretending to read the newspaper that I held with both hands. I got closer to the man while my heart was pounding. I looked him in the eye. He too, looked me directly in the eye. And he kept on looking at me as I was inching closer. As the train stopped, I got totally freaked out and I abandoned my plans. I got out of the train and sat at one of the benches in Kings Cross station platform, with my heart still pounding. I met Bef most of Friday evenings for a drink or two – he normally paid for them – at my local pub. On one of those Fridays, we were both standing at the bar counter facing each other. Once the bar got busier, I pushed myself into Bef. I slid my right hand, then my index and middle fingers into his inside jacket's pocket. Quickly and smoothly, I picked out his wallet. I dropped it and caught it with my left hand at the hem of his jacket. I went to the toilet. I found £80 in Bef's wallet. I took out a ten and a twenty-pound note and put them in my pocket. I went back to the bar and managed to slip Bef's wallet back inside one his outside pockets. From then on, I kept on pushing myself against Bef and pickpocketing him, every now and then. I was learning new skills and hoping, soon enough, I'd use them in the trains at St Pancras train station.

It isn't my history and I should steer clear of making judgment, but perhaps the English don't like the present. For whatever reasons, they choose to ignore present conditions and concentrate instead on the past. So I thought, when I passed Thornhill Square. The square was full of vans and trucks loaded with filming equipment. The technical crews were getting the lighting and camera tracks ready for, I presume, a scene or two for a period drama. I was seized by a sudden fit of depression when I saw, among all the people and trucks, the director's chair. The director was surrounded by his crew, standing behind him. The director, shouted, 'Camera! Action! Don't move!'

A man, wearing a black suit and a tie was sitting in a white bench, opposite a woman who was looking at him. The woman was wearing a black turtleneck mini dress and a necklace. They were surrounded by garden leaves. The man said, '... That was the day I photographed you, and you asked me to give you a year. Perhaps to test me, perhaps to weary me, or so you could forget. But time is important...'

'Cut!' The assistant director, shouted,

'What the fuck!' the director shouted,

The assistant director leaned in and said loudly, close to the director's right ear and into his hearing aid, 'He forgot his lines! He said, important...'

The director said, 'Oh! Not again. It is unimportant! But time is UNIMPORTANT! ...'

After Ritjana dumped me, I tried to avoid watching films about love. But perusing The Film Shop's shelves was painful because I had to read the films' synopsis at the back of the DVD covers. And on many occasions, I ended up reading about love. And so, most of the time I'd come out with films that I had seen before. And sometimes, I'd go home without renting any films, but once I was home, I'd remember 1, 2 or 3 things I knew about her. One early morning, I woke from a bad dream. A really bad dream. In my dream, I tried to engineer my own death by burying myself alive after the contract killer I hired hadn't turn up to shoot me outside The Film Shop at the sunrise. He was one of three contract killers I met. The other two not only refused but questioned me about the morality of suicide, even though I was offering them money to do it.

I carried on dreaming. My mother stood motionless behind my brother and me. Perhaps she was thinking about our absent father, who was fighting with the Eritrean Liberation Front (ELF) in the war of independence against Ethiopia. My brother spilt milk on the sand while we were eating our breakfast on the ground in our hut. Our black cat tried to lap up the milk but only for the sands to absorb it. My brother spilt sugar from the palm of his hand onto the black cat's fur. My mother shouted, 'Fire!' I ran and stopped by the door of our hut. Our neighbour's hut was on a fire and the sky was raining.

When I was a member of The Film Shop, I used the phone booth quite a lot after Virgin Media, my landline provider, cut off my landline because I hadn't paid my bills for months. I had a Pay as You Go Mobile phone, but it wasn't compatible with my hearing aid. Sometimes, I used to walk long distances to find a working kiosk. People were using them less and less, and as a result BT lost interest in their maintenance. One day, I saw more than a dozen of pigeons flying around me. I didn't pay much attention to them. But soon they began annoying me. They were literally following me, flying all over my head. I flailed my arms but to no avail. I took a refuge in a phone booth (KX100).

'... Please say your name again? Louder and slower!' I said

'ME-AANIE!' Said the TV license phone operator.

'Ok, Me-aanie. You see, I don't watch TV at all, so, why do I have to pay for a TV license?'

'I'm sorry. Anbad who — a TV ass to pay...'

'I am sorry. I cannot hear you. I live in my own. I cannot ask anybody to call you for me...'

'Im sooy...?

'I cannot afford to pay. I never watch TV. I only watch films. I borrowed money to buy my new TV, so I can watch films in a large screen...'

'YOU CAN pay in monthy...'

'I already pay £10 a month to watch films and you want me to pay for something I never use...'

'I DO NOT THINK I wee b ABLE HELP YOU...'

I slammed the handset on the phone and looked around. I saw hundreds of pigeons, literally, surrounding the phone booth and eating. I then saw a short and fat old man with a large belly and bald head, throwing food around, on the pavement. And when I tried to open the door, the man threw food into the phone booth. Dozens of pigeons entered the booth and began eating around my feet.

I wrote my first short story, *The Girl and the Cloud* over an existing film script. However, I forgot to delete the words "THE END" at the end of the short story. This was pointed out to me by a poet friend who told me that you don't write THE END in stories. This got me thinking, why do we always see the word THE END, written mostly in white on a black background when a film ends. Films don't end with the word THE END on black screen. After THE END, we still think about the film from its last frame and onwards, constructing an epilogue. We go back and forth about what happened and what should or could have happened and what we wished to have happened. In the process, we draw events to our own conclusion, that we may change many times over. So, perhaps there is no beginning either! An artist friend of mine once told me that her white canvas is never empty before she begins to paint. It is already populated with the mind's projections of images.

I got a new digital hearing aid. This hearing aid has a memory. It remembers to distinguish the human voice from the background noise around me. When it does so, it amplifies the voice and softens for example, the sounds in the street. As a result, my friendship with Bef became much closer. I could hear Bef more clearly when I walked with him in the streets and sometimes, I'd tease him and say, 'My hearing aid remembers you better than me.' Hearing through hearing aids is not as straight forward as putting on glasses. Perhaps I could compare it to filming. When shooting a film, recording sound, even on location, is relatively easy, recording images however, is more complicated when it comes to lighting. To simplify the difference in quality, between analogue hearing aids which I had in the past, and digital hearing aids, perhaps we can think of the difference between a VHS Camcorder and an HD camera. No matter how good the HD is, its image is still 2D flat. Some changes are great, some are fine, and some are not, I told myself, standing outside a corner shop after I bought a candle. I looked at The Film Shop, on the other side of the street. I lit the candle and began crossing the street. I struggled with the wind and rain to keep the flame alive. I protected the flame with my hands and my coat. Cars stopped and honked their horn. It took me 9 minutes! I put the candle on the pavement in front of the black door of The Film Shop. The flame died out. The Film Shop was converted to a grocery store and was called Desmond's. But that too, soon closed. I peeped through the horizontal tubes' security shutters. I saw an abandoned ice cream vendor freezer and scattered papers on the floor. I looked at the empty shelves all over the walls, then to my left where I used to stand before the desk and chat to Gabrielle, who stood behind it with her tiny but toned figure, her square-shaped beautiful face with thick red lips that once shouted; Haworth! Village of Haworth! I then looked straight at the flat dark wall with no door that would lead you down after a few steps to the Arthouse room. I was a member of The Film Shop for almost four years. And for two of those years, I used to go down to this room, practically every day, taking home with me three films a day; sometimes four or five, if the staff were in a generous mood. I knew this space so well I told myself, but does it recognise me? Spaces know no mercy. They just spit at your back as soon as you leave them. The relationship is entirely one-sided. Or, perhaps they love us silently. Perhaps that is why they keep dragging us to them, time and again by putting their spell on us, long before we even knew it.

II

Friday Past Midnight.

London, Islington, London, 2009.

On a Friday after midnight, Upper Street is busy with revelers. Negash, a man in his early twenties and looking drunk, walks past two young pretty girls, also seemingly drunk and eating kebabs. The two girls throw a glance at Negash and giggle.

Negash holds a small piece of a paper and stands alone next to a phone booth (KX100). Negash tries to hand the paper to a young passerby who barely throws him a glance. But he manages to stop another young passerby, who reads it, laughs out loud and walks away. Negash hands a £10 note to a homeless middle-aged man, covered in a blanket and holding a dirty worn-out black suitcase who shakes Negash's hands in gratitude. Negash hands him the paper. The homeless man reads it and disappears into the phone booth and emerges a few minutes later, holding a call card.

As Negash looks down at the house number, a young man in a city suite emerges from the basement flat. Negash looks away and walks back. Negash waits until the man disappears from his view, then walks down and rings the bell.

A middle-aged woman opens the door and let Negash in. Negash walks through the entrance room. In the room, there is a woman asleep on a two-seater sofa, covered in a blanket with only her bare feet visible. Another woman is sitting half asleep on a chair, covered to the neck, in front of a TV showing a foreign channel. A young brunette, tall and slightly plump with big breasts walks past Negash. Her body is covered with a large towel and her head is in a shower cap.

She is also holding a pair of high heeled shoes in one hand and knickers in the other. The woman puts the shoes and the other items on the floor and sits on the floor next to a radiator.

Negash sits on a double bed. Three girls in lingerie come into the room and stand in front of Negash; one is very young, blonde with tiny figure. Another has short hair and the third is the one he saw earlier wrapped in a towel. The girl with the towel asks Negash which girl he wants. Negash, signing, tells her that he is deaf. The girl switches off the music. Using her fingers, she gestures money. Negash shows her the back of the call card, it reads:

£60 = 30 mins, full service including massage.

£100 = 1hour, full service including massage.

£30 = Blowjob only.

Negash points at £60 and chooses the girl with the towel. When they are alone, Negash drops to his knees and hugs the girl for a long time. The girl, and after a long hesitation, strokes Negash's head gently. The girl hears loud sounds coming from outside. She beacons to Negash to go under the bed and walks out of the room.

One male police officer stands by the main exit door. Two other male officers check documents. The three girls, still in their lingerie, sit on the sofa next to the middle aged woman, who appears to be the madam. A woman officer looks at the madam, and says, 'You are under arrest on suspicion of human trafficking for sexual exploitation...'

In the morning, Negash wakes up and crawls out from under the bed. He opens the flat's door and walks up the stairs slowly. As he pushes the iron bar gate, he sees a young couple who seem to be living in the flat above. They are on their way out for a weekend trip. There are few bags on the pavement next to their Mini and a small dog on the back seat. Among those bags, there is one large brown recyclable Primark bag. Negash puts his head down and walks past the couple. He looks at the gated garden and then at the square's name: Gibson Square.

THE LITERARY CONFERENCE

I was waiting for V at Liverpool Street station, standing by the train door, anxiously trying to spot V's face among the afternoon rush hour crowd. I hadn't seen him for over a month, he had been on a poetry reading tour to eastern Europe where his last stop was Russia. Finally, V appeared dishevelled and unshaven and, apparently, with a hangover and unshaven face. After we took our seats, I asked, 'What is the conference about?'

'Shakespeare,' V said.

'What,' I said, 'I know nothing about Shakespeare.'

'Just make things up as you go along,' said V and looked away through the window.

It is my first ever conference, I told myself, and from all those writers, why, why Shakespeare?

It was V's idea to attend the conference. A week earlier, I got an email from him asking if I was free and that he'd be suggesting my name as a last-minute replacement for one delegate who got ill and therefore couldn't attend. I then exchanged a flurry of emails with V and the director of the conference. Both were concerned about my hearing, and according to the director they had never dealt with someone with my conditions before. I suggested to them if they'd be able provide me with radio aids then I should be fine. A FM system/radio aid is a small wireless receiver device that would be attached to my hearing aid in order for me to receive signals from a transmitter which would be worn by the speaker. But, they answered, because of the tight timeline they won't be able purchase the items. I then suggested if I could sit next to each person when they are talking because I could hear from my right ear where my hearing aid is if I sat close to the speaker. But I was told that was impractical. I was glad the director said that. I wrote that suggestion in an impulse. I couldn't have imagined moving my chair and sitting next to a delegate each time he/she speaks. I got this idea because I once attended a life drawing classes for three months, one day a week. In this course, there was a deaf woman who had the same condition as I; she was completely deaf in her left ear and used a hearing aid her in right ear. So, every time the teacher or a student spoke, the woman in question, used to walk and stand next to the teacher or the student and move her ear close to their mouths. The teacher or students were always feeling uncomfortable to the point that I felt they spoke less and less as the lessons went by.

Anyway, when the director suggested we could leave it for next time, I begged, persisted and insisted on attending the conference no matter what.

Shortly upon our arrival at our hotel, we were escorted by a communication team member to a nearby building. When we arrived, the evening performance had already begun. I didn't hear a word of it. There were two men in costumes performing a scene of one of Shakespeare's plays. I didn't ask V what it was about because I could still see he was lost in his own thoughts. Maybe he is in love again, I thought. So I was daydreaming or perhaps, thinking about a short story I was writing at that time – this I always do when such circumstances occur; I look and never see but think.

However and whatever it was, it was performed under a ruined building. I soon recognised the writer Janis who was sitting on the other side, opposite me, under one of the columns ruins. Janis was one of a few living writers I admired at that time. Her subject matter didn't interest me as much as her technique: I thought it was like having one single idea for a short story and overstretching it over a few pages, just like taking a chew gum line out of your mouth and then stretching it as far as you can without breaking it.

After the performance, all of us went to a restaurant. V, as usual sat on my right. There wasn't any kind of agreement between V and me to sit like this, but he more or less understood that I can only hear from my right ear and with the person being close to me. This wasn't without disadvantages, because, in a way, it was preventing me from meeting new people of my liking, making contacts, and exchanging ideas. Besides, on many occasions some people assumed we were partners. This was far from the truth: in fact, I'd always wished to strangle V and whoever I depended on to hear on occasions like this with my bare hands.

After the dinner, V, Huifen, Janis, and I sat at the hotel bar. After a few drinks, my shyness evaporated. I told Janis how much I loved and appreciated her work. I also said that one of my Arabic language students who was herself a writer bought her book upon my recommendation, and my student told me after that Janis was an idiot and in need for psychiatric help. In an instant, everyone's jaws dropped while looking at each other. I paused a bit longer than usual, and then added my student told me a few months later that Janis was now growing on her. Janis laughed out loud, and so we all did.

On the first day of the conference and as soon as I entered the hall, I knew I wouldn't hear much, if anything at all, because the hall was large and the ceiling very high. The delegates' voices will disappear before they reach my hearing aid. I sat next to V, facing the moderator. There were 25 of us at a round table. I looked at my copy of the delegates brochure on the table. As I leafed through the pages, my emotions were awe and fear. Some of the delegates were eminent professors, some highly respected Shakespearean scholars, some were well known writers and poets. And then I saw my name and my bio written on a thick light-golden paper cut to fit over the delegate's bio I replaced. The paper was clipped neatly with a large gold coloured paperclip. I turned the paper over and read the absent delegate's bio. I was petrified; the man wrote 17 poetry collections, 3 novels, 4 plays, 4 essay collections and his own autobiography.

The moderator, a professor, began to speak and soon was followed by other delegates. It was when V spoke that I realised the delegates were introducing themselves. When it was my turn, I said my name and that I wrote short stories and stopped abruptly – there was nothing for me to add. I only wrote one short story, and it was published online on a website ran by V. And then I looked on my left. The delegate introduced himself as a journalist and then the delegates carried on introducing themselves one after another.

The professor began talking about Shakespeare – I presume, because I kept on hearing over and over, the words: Shakespeare, Shake, and Shakear, Shakespeare, Shake, Kebare, Shebear, Bear, Beer, Sha, Share, Shake, Shakare...

The writer who wrote 7 books presented his paper on Shakespeare as the brochure promised. I heard no word of it. Afterwards, so the brochure said, everyone was free to share his opinion of what the writer said. So the delegates who wished to speak were putting their hands up and spoke at the invitation of the moderator. As the delegates were speaking, I noticed a Japanese woman on my left; according to the brochure, she worked at the Royal Shakespeare Company. I thought she reminded me of a certain Japanese actress I admired but then I thought of Kurosawa. Earlier, I also heard one of the delegates utter the words 'Shakespeare in translation'. I was determent to take part. I put my hand up. The chair professor pointed at me. I said, 'A long time ago I watched the film Throne of Blood by Kurosawa. It was in Japanese with English subtitles. There were many Shakespearean motifs... Some critics thought it was the best ever film adaptation despite Kurosawa not using a single word of Shakespeare... He used fog, wind, trees, mist...' I saw some delegates nodding their heads. And with total confidence, I added, 'Kurosawa showed that, even without words, Shakespeare would still triumph...'

'Well said,' said the professor, nodding. I could hear him because he addressed me directly. Everyone was looking at me in approval. Many were nodding their heads at me in approval too. I felt confident. I felt I owned the hall.

At the dinner, I was sitting opposite Janis who was sitting next to Jennica. I was surprised by the Janis's coldness – she ignored me at lunch time and now wasn't even looking at me, talking to Jennica as if I wasn't there. I thought about what I said to her last night and if I said anything bad. I didn't. All what I said was in praise of her work. I even told her how much I admired her work and that she deserves The Booker prize. She had nodded and said, you are right.

I was left alone. I was smiling or laughing as soon as I saw one of them smiling or laughing. Then I thought, I thought that writers were, perhaps, a bit more conscious of life, or at least theoretically. Of love, pain, and joy. Of power, weakness, and failure. I thought if Janis saw my hearing aid, she would be conscious of my hearing loss. Perhaps, she would see my hearing aid and would take the lead to talk to me in a way I'd be able to hear her. After all, I am hearing people's problems, as one friend, a writer, once said to me. But then Jennica, who was a specialist in Shakespeare, said looking directly at me, 'S., please entertain us about Shakespeare.'

'I know nothing about Shakespeare,' I said

Jennica and Janis looked at each other.

'But wait...,' I said, 'Yes... I remember this funny story. I read somewhere that an Arab dictator once proclaimed Shakespeare as an Arab writer. The dictator explained that the name Shakespeare was in fact a combination of two names: Sheikh – an honorific title in Arabic – and Zubair, a proper noun. Together, they are pronounced as Sheikhzubair. The English couldn't pronounce Sheikhzubair so they called him Shakespeare...'

I waited for their laughs. Shit! You idiot! I wanted to shout. They didn't find it funny.

Later on, most of us, the delegates, were at a local bar. I was in the beer garden, which made my hearing easier – they were very few people around – with V and Janis. V asked me why I don't show much in my writing and he thought that I was kind of a minimalist. I said, 'Bresson...' then I abruptly stopped. I looked at Janis and then shrugged, and said, 'I don't know.' I didn't know why I stopped my sentence short.

I normally go on talking about my ideas non-stop with V. Perhaps I didn't want to yell out my techniques. Perhaps, I didn't like Janis. Or perhaps I didn't want to sound pretentious in front of someone I now disliked.

I was at the hotel's canteen for breakfast and saw Jennica, who politely asked me to join her. I put my breakfast tray on Jennica's table and sat opposite her. Jennica looked at me and then politely said, 'I heard that you lived in a refugee camp...' Oh not again, I told myself, she must have spoken to Huifen. Huifen always introduced me to her friends as someone who has been to two refugee camps. She would say it like this: This is S. S. lived in two refugee camps, and repeats with her fingers, TWO REFUGEE CAMPS.

Jennica asked me politely if storytelling was important in refugee camps. But before I answered her, one of the delegates whose name I didn't know sat at our table with his breakfast tray. He talked to us but spoke very fast. I didn't hear him or Jennica, so naturally I thought of Jennica's question. And if I had answered her, I'd have started by saying that after food and water there lurks the boredom. At the early stages in the refugee camp life, the entire population is out of work; they must have had too much free time for new experiences. A new reality in a new space. I don't remember much about how the adults thought or spent their time then, but we, the kids – I was 8 or 9 then – were running and playing around as though nothing had happened.

At the conference's morning session, Jennica presented her film, shot in a refugee camp in an Arab country. It was, the brochure said, a documentary of refugee camp productions of Lear. After the film finished, Jennica talked about her film at length, and then the delegates were putting their hands up to share their ideas. As one delegate was talking, I thought of the children that I saw in Jennica's film, walking among the thousands of white tents. I put my hands up. But another delegate spoke so again I thought…

One morning, we woke up in the refugee camp. It was summer. Monday early morning around 6 AM in Kassala, Sudan. We heard knocks and shouts outside our yard's door. My grandfather opened the door. A number of Sudanese soldiers burst in. They ordered us collect all our belongings and said that they were taking us to a nice place. My grandfather pleaded with them to spare us because his son's wedding was to take place on Friday, the same week. The seating and catering arrangements had been organised around the yard. One more week, grandfather said. My uncle wasn't deported with us. He was staying that night with friends in a different part of the city, close to his beloved; this area wasn't raided by the authorities. The soldiers refused my grandfather's pleas and told us to collect our belongings or they will do it themselves. My grandfather pleaded again for one more week. He then asked the soldiers to allow me and my younger brother to go and tell my granduncle and his family, who lived in a different area, that we were being deported. My brother and I approached the main road. We saw the whole street lined with armed soldiers so no Eritrean residents would try escape. One of the soldiers stopped and asked us where we were going. I showed him our pass. But he looked at me and then at the bandage on my head, and said, refugees and troublemakers. No, I said, pointing at the back of my head, I was walking with friends last week. When we passed a tree, I saw a bird on the branches. I stopped and picked up a stone. I threw the stone to catch the bird. I missed. As I was walking back to join my friends, the stone fell back and hit me. The soldiers roared in laughter. One of them shouted: *idiot*, and allowed us through. The journey to the camp was long. We arrived at the camp after midnight. Our lorry stopped in front of a hut and so did the other lorries. It was all mysterious and dark seeing the headlights all around us as if they were stars fallen on the ground from the starlit sky...

As the delegate finished another one spoke...

...In the first morning in the camp, we woke up and found the lorries has mysteriously disappeared. While we were arranging our belongings, I heard grandpa say to a passerby, *no it isn't a dream!* There were thousands of identical huts surrounding us. All the huts were newly built in a flat dry land. We were given free tinned food. The authorities gave us new clothes, though they were second hand western clothes, some were heavy coat jackets but no one wore them because temperature exceeded 40C. We met our new neighbours. We brought our water from the nearby river. During the day we, the children, played on the streets, swam in the river, went on expeditions to the outskirts of the camp. During the night, we retired to our huts and we only met our nearest neighbours, surrounding our huts. But we missed TV. In Kassala we didn't have TV so we used to go to our Sudanese neighbours' houses to watch TV at night. The Sudanese neighbours were always welcoming. We, the children, met outside our huts during the moonlight nights and told each other stories. Soon we ran out of stories. Two brothers built a shallow card box with a worn-out plastic sheet taped on one side. They made two cut outs of a cat and a dog, each held by a long thread. They put a lantern at the back of the box. We saw the silhouette of the cat and the dog on the plastic sheet. The dog ran after the cat barking, woof, woof, and the cat ran away shouting, meow, meow. Left, right. Meow, meow. Woof, woof. Left, right. Right, left. After a month or so, a new group of refugees arrived. We found a family who came with a TV. But we had no electricity. We found someone who had an electricity generator. In one evening, everything was set. The whole neighbourhood children were sitting in front of the TV. But there was no reception. We kept on changing channels to no avail. One child held the indoor aerial and moved it away from the TV. We saw a flicker of a newsreader. We shouted, stop, stop. But the image disappeared in an instant. We changed the channels. We moved the areal. We saw a flicker of cartoon images. We all screamed. Cartoon! Cartoon. The cartoon disappeared. We moved the aerial left to right, right to left, up and down, down and up. We did this all night long for days on end without us seeing any images apart from a flicker here and a flicker there. We gave up. But we found her. The storyteller. She was an old woman, very old, living on her own. Every night she sat outside her hut and, we sat surrounding her under the moonlight. She told us story after story after story. Night after night after night...

As V began speaking, I had the feeling, I'd be next. I knew what I'd be talking about. It'd be about the storyteller and one of her stories. I was sitting with my hands folded on the table, deep in my thoughts. V was resting on his back on the chair. I managed to capture a few words of what V said. Such as, Virgil... Different... A Roman poet... Repetition, exile, time... Repetition, I thought, repetition. V stopped talking, the moderator signed me to talk.

'Time becomes before and after,' I said, 'Time is cut to before and after. Time ceases to be a circle. If time is put into series with respect to this cut, then there are forms that cannot return that are consigned to remain past for ever and there are forms that return with the cut that are relived with it. When Hamlet uttered 'Time is out of joint'; it was a caesura. It was to throw time out of joint, to make the sun explode, to throw oneself into volcano.

The I is fractured. The self is divided according to the temporal series but finds a common descendant in the man without a name, without a family, without qualities, without self or I. All is repetition in the temporal series. The past is in itself repetition as is the present. Two different modes repeating each other. Repetition isn't a historical fact but a historical condition under which something new is produced. We produce something new only on condition that we repeat. No repetition is the same. Only difference returns. No difference without repetition, no repetition without difference. The difference in itself and the repetition for itself… Repetition of—'

I abruptly stopped. I couldn't utter the next word or perhaps I didn't have any clue about the next word or sentence. 'I cannot continue,' I said.

Everyone was looking at me with their mouths half open. I felt hands patting me on the back. It felt bad. I wanted to hide under the table.

At lunch time, I told the director of the conference that I decided to cut my stay short. I was supposed to stay for night and the following day. I thought it was better to leave with V, who was going that afternoon. I was embarrassed about what had happened, and I didn't feel confident to stay on. I couldn't bear a dinner where I may end up alone.

On our way to the train station, V and I went to the city's cathedral. Inside, we stopped in front of a painting. I asked V, 'Who are those three characters?'

'The three wise men…'

'Wise men of who?'

'The three kings,' said V, 'Don't you know them?'

'No…,' I said.

'I thought you liked T.S Eliot. They are his subject in The Journey of the Magi …'

I looked at V. I have never seen him that distant. 'Look,' I said, 'When I read western literature… I pass on many of the references… Sometimes I don't have time to read a referenced books or even google… As far as I am concerned, if I understand the meaning then fine, and if I don't, I move on to the next…'

We then went to the Monastery. V received a flurry of texts messages, and said, 'I need time by myself… I need to write something.'

I walked around admiring the Cloisters. And at the same time, I wondered if V had done it on purpose, uttering the words 'Difference and repetition' just before I gave my speech. I had read Gilles Deleuze's *Difference and Repetition* more than 10 times and read many more books that claim to interpret it. I liked *Difference and Repetition* the first time I read it and thought I understood it. The second time I read it, I understood less. And then strangely, the more I read it the less I understood. Still, I thought I knew the book to the point that if someone uttered the words 'Difference or repetition', I would involuntarily remember a passage or two from the book. I believe I told this to V. And that was why I was a bit suspicious that he did it in purpose. I clenched my fists and resolved to punch V on the face. Am I a parrot, I asked myself, a Deleuzian parrot? If so, perhaps I am no different than the Shakespearean parrots. Those actors or the ones who recite Shakespeare by heart and who will understand nothing. I am a parrot, I shouted, and so are Shakespearean actors.

'Are you ok?' V said.

'No, I am all right,' I said, still clenching my fists.

'I am sad…' V said

'I can see that,' I said, unclenching my fists.

THE CASTLE OF GONDAR

'Ah! And where are your parents originally from?' Claudia asked.

'Eritrea,' I said

'That is exactly what I thought,' with a beaming smile, said Claudia. Claudia then told me she was a photographer and that she thought I had a handsome face, and she would like to photograph me.

'I don't mind,' I said, 'But for what propose?'

'For now, I don't know,' She adjusted her oversized spectacles, 'Maybe for my art projects or else for adverts in magazines or brochures.'

'And what is there for me?' I said, while looking at her face then at her hair; she had a high top fade hair cut .

'I will give you large and high quality print copies. And,' said Claudia, 'I promise, I will only use your pictures upon your permission.'

'Ok...' I said, then I got dragged away by my colleague, Kjerstin, into the Italian regions and Campania pavilion. The pavilion was packed. It was decorated in colourful advertising boards about airlines or cruise ships, tourist beauty spots, or landmarks. There were girls wearing period costumes made of the silk from San Leucio. We saw locally made handicrafts, we tasted sweets and chocolates, and wines from the Samnium and Irpinia regions; we ate bits of pizzas; we chatted to Italian tour operators and airlines and shipping companies' representatives.

In the late afternoon, I met Claudia outside the exhibition. We walked around a very long terraced, decayed cascade fountain, though there was no water. Claudia told me, the fountain was inaugurated in 1940. In the inauguration, she said, a symphony was performed while the water jets of those 24 circular fountains were synchronized with the music. I stopped by a large and elegant building. It is the swimming pool, Claudia said. I asked her about the piece of artwork on the wall. It is called African Rhythms, Claudia answered, and said, pointing at the figures, it portrays a scene of everyday life in an African village. As we walked on a long avenue of four rows of palm trees Claudia told me she worked as a cruise ship photographer. She worked on the ship for seven months a year and for the remaining months she was either a freelancer doing special commissions around Italy's tourist resorts or doing her own art projects.

When we turned to the left, I saw a pond. We walked to the pond, which had greenish water with a few ducks and swans floating. Claudia began setting up her camera. I saw a small three stories high building that looked like a mini medieval castle, and for a moment it seemed to be floating on the pond. Claudia asked me to stand at the bank of the pond. I looked at the castle again. No, it wasn't floating, in fact, it was built on arched stilts and columns rising from the bottom of the pool. The castle had empty door frames and window frames, and the lower parts of the doorways and windows were filled with wild grass. Claudia adjusted my tie and then, looking at my badge where my name, Tesfaye Gebremichael, was written above our company name "Nomad Exodus". She said, 'So what do you do?'

'I am a tour operator,' I said.

'Oh, Great!' Claudia said, then she asked me to take off my badge and to look directly to look at her camera. She adjusted my chin with her hand; her fingers were really soft. She took a few shots with the castle behind me and then checked her camera view finder. I looked at the castle again. I saw a black man in white dress, standing, framed by one of the windows of the second floor. But he disappeared in a flash. Claudia asked me to rest my chin on my left hand and place the other hand on my waist. She took more shots while moving closer and closer to me. I turned my head to the left again. I saw a man in an Ethiopian Gabi dress and a child wearing a white dress standing at the arched doorway on the first floor of the castle.

'Don't move your head,' Claudia shouted.

Claudia crouched on bended knee and asked me to tilt my head backward and relax, with my hands at my sides. She took more shots. I saw a few passers-by standing nearby and looking at us. I asked Claudia if she knew anything about the building. It looks strange and out of place, I said, compared to the other building on this site. Claudia told me, this castle is very popular as a shooting set for movies and TV soap operas and that she once did stills for a feature film that had scenes shot here, and then added, *its name is castle of Gondar*, while replacing her camera lens with a larger one.

'What!' I said, 'My mother is from Gondar...'

'Where is Gondar?' Claudia asked, while adjusting the lens.

'Ethiopia.'

'I thought you were from Eritrea,' said Claudia, while focusing her lens.

'Well, my father is from Eritrea and my mother from Ethiopia.'

'Ah...' She asked me to crouch down on one knee, then took a few steps back and herself crouched down on knee. Some onlookers stopped briefly to look at us or take photos of us taking photos.

Afterwards Claudia and I sat by the pond. I asked Claudia about her work and tried to concentrate on what she was saying while looking at the castle's arches then the windows. I was hoping to see that man in white dress again. He reminded me of my deceased uncle Tesfaye. At our home in Gothenburg, there is a black & white photograph of my uncle, wearing Gabi dress, hung on one of the living room walls. He was the beloved brother of my mother and she named me after him. I met him just once in Gondar. Gondar. I visited Gondar 21 years ago. I could remember some scenes from Gondar. Walking with my uncle. I was 5 years old, a very tiny little boy. *My little sweet boy*, my uncle says. My uncle buys me sweets from a street vendor. A yard. I run in a dusty road.

'... I like portrait photography,' said Claudia, 'I like to photograph the present. The people... very present... live in. Our time...to blur the background so... as possible... a timeless quality as memory...'

A young girl, wearing a green dress. The girl is taller and bigger than me.

'... True...photograph becomes past... act is in the present...' Claudia carried on, 'I love the sea and the sky... photographing in the ocean linear is paid commercial work...'

A bright green dress. The girl looks four or five years older than me. She has a long soft black hair and brown skin.

'... to investigate the sea and the sky...never tinted by time... They are as timeless as the Greek myths....'

The girl drags me away from my mother. The girl smooths my head with her left hand. My left hand grabs her green dress. We are running around a large open space. A street. No, a yard. No, a street.

'... Do you know Clio?' asked Claudia.

'Clio! Who?'

'Never mind,' said Claudia, 'I like talking to you.'

After a brief silence, Claudia said, 'Since you have roots from Gondar, I would like you to come with me to an art show. You won't believe it but it's titled The Castle of Gondar.'

We agreed to meet by the pond at 8 in the morning. Claudia wanted to take a few more shots of me in the morning sun against the Castle. Then we could walk to the gallery. Claudia said, I love to walk.

At 8 in the morning, I walked along the palm trees avenue, looking up at the branches and leaves. The trees were tall and imposing. I had a bit of a hangover from the night before, I drank a lot at the hotel bar with Kjerstin and my boss, Tobias, and a couple of Argentinian delegates. Tobias drinks a lot on such occasions. I saw him kissing Kjerstin. Tobias was married with two children. Anyway, I sent a message to Tobias saying I was sick and switched off my mobile. I also put DON'T DISTURB on my room's door. I don't think they will make a fuss. No. Kjerstin suffers from PTSD and I have been listening to her, to all the details of her life, all the time. Tobias is dyslexic and I have always helped and supported him. I think I will get away with this one. I don't think he will make any fuss.

I saw Claudia approaching on the far side of street. I walked towards her while zigzagging between the palm trees' trunks. We hugged. I thought she looked even prettier than yesterday and told her how pretty she was; I was struck by her wide lips. But Claudia gave me a stern and serious stare. I was taken aback by her response but I let it go. We walked to the pond. Claudia took a few shots and then we headed to the city's centre.

As we walked, Claudia told me about Naples, about Vesuvius and about Naples's historical port. And she also said that though she dislikes the fascists, she couldn't help but admire what marvellous architectural creations they had left behind. Claudia then went on describing the open theatre at Mostra d'Oltremare as one of best examples of rationalist architecture. It was, she said, modelled and inspired by the architectural models of Greek and Roman theatres scattered around Magna Graecia areas. Rationalist architecture, Claudia added, thrived after Mussolini's call in the 1920s for a Fascist style. The architects built many buildings in Italy inspired by past architectural glories... Mussolini had a link to Asmara, I wanted to say to Claudia. But Claudia continued, Fascist Italy spent much of the 1920s excavating imperial Rome. Theatres and Forums were seen for the first time in 1500 years, Italy's glorious past had been rediscovered. The new architecture should somehow reflect that, Mussolini declared. Mussolini. My father told me about Mussolini. My father is Asmarino. My father always talks about Asmara. Mussolini had a direct impact in the second revival of Italian colonialism of Eritrea, I know that. We entered a long, dark tunnel, with me walking behind Claudia as the pavement was narrow, just about wide enough for one person. When we got out of the tunnel, I looked at Claudia's dirty white Converse shoes and black ankle socks with her tapered black trousers ending at her calves. They were tight at the waist, making her bum very rounded.

Man, she is that beautiful. But dare I tell her that? When we passed Piazza Sannazaro, I noticed how beautiful the square was with its tall palm trees particularly striking. Those trees weren't much different in hight from the palm trees at Mostra d'Oltremare. Those palm trees. The trees at The Independence Avenue in Asmara. My book about Asmara. My father's Christmas's gift. The book has many pictures of The Independence Avenue. A street in Asmara that changed its name when one colonial ruler replaced another: It was Mussolini Avenue in the Italian period. Queen Victoria Avenue when the British took over. Emperor Haile Selassie Avenue when the British gave Eritrea to Haile Selassie. National Avenue when the Derg overthrow Haile Selassie. Independence Avenue when Eritrean rebels liberated Eritrea.

'... and this is'—Claudia pointed at a fountain with statues and animals and aquatic plants, positioned on a rock in the centre of the square—'The statue of the Parthenope, one of the sirens. According to Greek legend, Parthenope killed herself by throwing herself into the sea. Her lifeless body was washed off at shores of Naples—'

'Why did she kill herself?' I asked

'Because she wasn't able to seduce Odysseus with her songs.'

We arrived at a modern art gallery in central Naples. The exterior of the gallery seemed to have been newly refurbished, the frames of the doors and the huge windows newly installed in rusty, brown metal. Apart from the receptionist, there was no one in the gallery. Perhaps it was too early. On the front wall at the left of the entrance, there was the artist's statement. However, it was in Italian, so I couldn't read it. But Claudia stood next to me and translated it for me to English. She said, 'It is about the history of Mostra d'Oltremare. "Our research begins with a documentary photograph of a dead tree. The dead tree name is the tree of welwel. It was transported to Naples. The show also follows the story of 56 people who were brought to Italy from the Italian colonies to participate in the exhibition as... as exhibition items. They were employed... On a contractual basis. Their task was to live in the indigenous village built for them on the fair grounds. Also they produced artefacts and handcrafts from their traditional cultures during the exhibition hours... The exhibition was closed. One month after the opening after Italy entered World War II in June 1940. Due to the war, the Italian ports were closed. The 56 actors were forced to remain in Italy. After 1944 the group was still in Italy. Nobody knows what happened to them. Even after at the end of the war..."'

As exhibition items, I murmured. The first picture I saw was black and white, possibly of an Eritrean man. In the picture, he is in his tribal clothes wearing a white turban. He is standing next to a makeshift hut and on his left there is a resting camel, and between them a small tree. He is being looked at by an Italian family. Then another photograph of two men on white turban sitting on peaked hut structure. They are busy covering the peak with thatches. I took a step back. The picture was beautiful. I saw Claudia looking at a large stand with two freestanding framed black and white photographs of a dead tree. In the first photograph, there was a dead tree on an old truck which I assumed was a military transportation truck. On the second, there were two black men handling the tree, standing in the same truck. Again it was with an Italian caption. I asked Claudia about it. Claudia said, 'The pictures were taken in Somalia. It says, it is the historical tree of welwel... It was the tree from where the Italian troops fired their first shot on their way to Occupy Ethiopia... December 5, 1934. The tree travelled a long journey through Ogaden and Benadir, to Mogadishu. It says, it is a great relic and will be exhibited at Mostra d'Oltremare. After that it would be moved to the Colonial Museum in Rome...'

Claudia walked away and I looked at another photograph on the wall. It was a photograph of a Neapolitan child, perhaps four or five years of age, wearing a white short dress; she is standing holding her father's hand – he is behind her, wearing a full black suit, waistcoat, and a fedora hat. There are two other men standing next to him, both also in full suits. They are all looking at the back of a black man dressed in a knee-length white shirt and matching trousers, with a white Gabi placed over his shoulders and upper body. The girl and the men are looking at the man as if he is something strange and unfamiliar. The black man who is standing behind a newly built hut is taking a step forward and is about to step out of the frame. He is looking directly at the camera, with his mouth slightly open. And another photograph of a castle. The castle looked exactly the same as the castle on the pond at Mostra d'Oltremare. It had a caption. I asked Claudia. Claudia walked over, and said, 'It is a faithful reproduction of Fasilides bath from the Castle of Gondar...'

'It is from Gondar?' I asked Claudia.

Claudia nodded.

'The same castle as—?'

Claudia nodded.

'Is this really the same place where the Mediterranean tourism exchange is being held?'

Claudia nodded and walked to look at another picture. I looked at another picture. A coloured photograph of a child sitting on the ground next to flowers of blue roses in long green stems with long barbed wire installed behind; she is wearing a red jumper and a yellow skirt.

Claudia and I walked out of the gallery. In silence, we sat at a bench in a park. Then I lay on my back looking at the blue sky and Claudia looked away at the people walking by.

'I was born in Naples but I live in Bologna,' Claudia said. 'Have you ever been to Bologna?'

'No, never.'

'So you have never visited the Eritrean festival in Bologna?'

'No, I've never heard of it.'

'It is a festival that was founded by the Eritrean diaspora in Bologna in the seventies. Would you like to go to the festival this year with me?'

'I don't know.' I shrugged.

'I don't think you like me,' Claudia said.

'Why?' I said with a half-smile.

'For being an Italian.'

'I haven't thought of that.'

'Look, this past is unfamiliar to me,' said Claudia.

'I don't know much either.'

'Tell me what you think,'

'About what?'

'About what we saw,' said Claudia.

'I don't know how or what to think right now,' I said, and

looked at my phone to check the time.

'Shall we meet tomorrow again at the same place, by the castle?' Claudia asked.

'Yeah, why not?'

'At 8.'

'Yeah, at 8,' I said.

Soon after I as I left Claudia, I found myself walking in a narrow street. I went into a corner shop to buy cigarettes. I came out and saw an African man begging outside the shop with his right hand extended and open. As I was handing him a few Euros, I tried to look at his fingers to see if there were any signs of burns on his finger tips. But he closed his hand in an instant, shoved it into his pocket, and thanked me. I heard those immigrants burn their finger tips before they arrive to Europe, to avoid being fingerprinted upon their arrival on Italian soil, so they won't be sent back to Italy if they ever leave to another European country. But I saw his palm: it was rough. I heard it from Lorikan. Lorikan said they have calloused hands. Hands. They are so many of them. Almost at every street corner. A corner here. A corner there. I saw Eritreans here. Ethiopians there. But they never extended their hands to me. They are avoiding me. They look like me. They are avoiding my sight. Because of the way I dress. Because they are too proud to ask someone who looks like them. Maybe they don't want me to see their burnt fingers. I don't know. I really don't know I want to know. But that man in a white Gabi. His left outstretched arm. The white fabric fitting tightly along the arm to the wrist. The back of his hand protruding from the fabric ending at his wrist. That man. He looks like my uncle Tesfaye or maybe not but their Gabi looks exactly the same. No, the man doesn't look like my uncle. Their dress looks the same. My uncle looks directly at the camera. With both hands visible from the white fabric ending at his wrist. This man is turning to his left side. The man's photograph was taken in the early 1940s, my uncle's photo in the mid-1970s. Uncle is happy; this man is anxious. Maybe he is wondering why he is there. As if. As if. No, maybe he is regretting his contract, or maybe he is saying something, something in a language neither the cameraman nor the people who were looking at him understand.

At a restaurant, I didn't eat what I ordered for lunch. Instead I drank a glass of Aperol Spritz. When I saw a black man begging by the window, I felt the weight of my skin colour. My colour. Not that I never paid attention to it, no, of course not. Sweden is known for its neutrality and liberalism, yet racism exists around many sections of the society. It is no big deal to me. It never affected me that much, I have a loving family, friends from Iran, Bosnia, Ethiopia, Eritrea. A couple of my best friends are white Swedish. It isn't easy to find a job, the job of my desire – For people like me. I only landed my job because the company was about to expand its operations in the near future to Kenya, Ethiopia, South Africa and Namibia. I have never had problem in Naples when it comes to my skin. I don't know. Maybe I dress well. Or maybe I am professional in dealing with people. But I know. I am beginning to see the African men and women differently now. Not the same way when I saw them on the first day of my arrival. The men and women who arrived by the sea. I am not saying I am beginning to identify with them. No, it is to do with how the Neapolitans feel about my presence.

I am Swedish. No. I am Eritrean. No. I am Ethiopian. No. I am Swedish Eritrean Ethiopian. Am I European? I don't know if I am or not. But what do the Italians see when they see me? I should never ask myself this question. But do they think of those immigrants when they see me? I am not a beggar. But I wanted to say how are you in Tigrinya or Amharic today to the Eritreans and Ethiopians I saw today. Or are you ok?

I finished my Aperol. I was feeling good and calm and my hangover seemed to have gone. I ordered another one. I looked around me and saw all the Italian faces, young and old, men and women, busy eating their lunch. At the far corner, there was a lonely women eating her lunch. I saw her picking up her glass of water and drinking in one go. She had a long neck. I followed her to her last sip of her glass. He neck was curved upon the last sip of water. Her neck looked like animal neck. A horse's neck. That clear glass. Water. Water, horses, donkeys, father said. The Italian horses and Eritrean donkeys. The one my father told me. The Eritrean soldiers fought alongside Italian colonisers to occupy Ethiopia. The soldiers advanced towards Ethiopia and arrived at a river. If there were about 50,000 Italian soldiers riding 50,000 horses. And about 100,000 Eritrean soldiers riding 100,000 donkeys. The Eritrean soldiers will be marching in front. Of course. When all arrived at the river, the Italian soldiers drank first and perhaps washed too; then the Italian horses, and after that the Eritrean donkeys. And then finally the Eritrean soldiers drank. But then what the Eritrean soldiers were doing while waiting. I asked my father this question. The Eritrean soldiers must still have been thirsty. Though, I am not sure if it was true. But I remember mother laughing. She said the Eritrean soldiers who fought alongside Italians were collaborators. *You wanted our Asmara* father said. When Emperor Haile Selassie arrived back to Addis after five years of exile. My father roared in laughter. He said *you wanted our Asmara*. Five years in exile in UK, then Haile Selassie arrived back after the Italian occupation ended. *After five years* said my mother. Haile Selassie saw what the Italians left behind, and Haile Selassie said the Italian should have stayed five more years. But why? Why? To finish what they started, to finish building roads and houses. *You wanted our Asmara* father said. My father is Asmarino. Anybody who is born and bred in Asmara is called Asmarino. My father is proud of Asmara. My mother always took the delight in annoying father, she always said *you never built it yourselves. The Italians built it for you*. My father said *it is ours. Ours. They built it in our land. We don't care. Ours.*

The young waitress brought me my second Aperol without ice or orange, I asked her why.

'Because... Because we,' in broken English the waitress said, 'No ice and orange.'

'I am not drinking this. It looks awful,' I said loudly.

Her boss seemed to have heard me, and, he came to my table with Neapolitan exaggerated expressions hand gestures and from this I gathered he was asking me to leave. And when I saw all the diners were looking at me, I slammed 50 Euros on the table – my lunch and drinks would had only have cost around 20 Euros – and left, shouting, '30 Euros for her!'

I took a taxi to the fair. I was sitting on the driver's side in the passenger's seat at the rear. After a while, I found it uncomfortable because the driver had pushed his seat back cramping my space, so I slid over to the other side. However, this wasn't the best position to see the sea to my left. We drove past the main port, the same port where the 56 actors must have arrived at before they were transported to Mostra d'Oltremare. The child. That child sitting behind the blue roses. Was she hiding behind the flowers away from the spectators? Or was she playing hide and seek with other children before the photographer spotted her? Before he aimed his lens on her. Where is she now? She looked 5 years old. The same age I arrived in Gottenborg. 5 years old. My mother met my father met in Nairobi, Kenya, they had both arrived there as refugees: Father ran away while fighting for EPLF in the Eritrean war of independence; mother was an air hostess in Ethiopian Airlines. She quit her job after the Ethiopian regime the Derg led by Mengistu Haile Mariam killed her father, who was an academic. Derg killed thousands of students and academics. When I was a child, I spoke Amharic with my mother and Tigrinya with my father. Two years after our arrival to Sweden, we all began speaking in Swedish at the house. I don't know why. Maybe to learn the language quicker. I speak Amharic better than Tigrinya but I can neither read or write on either languages. Amharic and Tigrinya have an incredible range of consonants. Each consonant has its own vowel. I could never get past writing my own name. Tesfaye. Te Tu Ti Ta Te Tê To. Ee Eu Ei Ea Ee Eê Eo. Se Su Si Sa Se Sê So. Fe Fu Fi Fa Fe Fê Fo. Ae Au Ai Aa Ae Aê Ao. Ye Yu Yi Ya Ye Yê Yo. Ee Eu Ei Ea Ee Eê Eo. I began reading Ethiopian and Eritrean history when I was 15. I know so much about Swedish and European histories. I read a lot about Ethiopian history but less so of Eritrean history. There are very few books about Eritrean history. Most of what I know came from my father's memory. And what he remembered came from his father and mother. Great grandfather and great grandmother. And to tell the truth, I am. Sometimes, I feel guilty because I am prouder of my mother's country. No, I never told my father. No. Ethiopia is the only nation in Africa not to be colonised. Yes, of course it only was occupied by Italy for 5 years. *We were occupied and you were colonised*, my mother used to correct my father.

I arrived on time at our pavilion with no fuss from my boss. He and I left Kjerstin, because she speaks a bit of Italian, at our stand to give flyers and talk to other operators while we both went to participate in an 'Incoming workshop'. The Incoming workshop hosts international buyers and Italian tour operators. We sat on a desk with a Swedish flag, put by the organisers, on our table, and an Italian tour operator/s sitting facing us. In two hours we successfully negotiated and bought 10 large group tours to Sardinia and Palermo, 45 a group to Capri, secured 7 of 8 per group tours in Puglia, and 50 a group tour to Naples for a period ranging between 2 weeks and a month. However, when I heard one of the Italians utter the number 56, I said, '56! Why 56?'

My boss tapped me on my hips. A sign to shut up or calm down.

'Because we only have 56 rooms,' said the hotelier.

'Ah! Ok,' I said and looked at the hotelier. He was a middle aged man. He was handsome with pushed back black soft hair, tanned skin and freshly shaved face, smelling of wonderful scents. His neck was encircled by a blue with white dots silk scarf. His scarf. A symbol of a perfect seller. I guess. A perfect negotiator. A perfect exhibiter. To exhibit items on contractual basis. The 56. Was there an Italian tour operator who negotiated their contracts in Eritrea and Ethiopia? By whom? By whom? Which companies? After all, it wouldn't be hard to argue his grandfather or even his father might have been here, on these premises. I am tempted to ask but...

Next morning I woke late with another hangover. I drank a lot; it was final night party. I decided not to meet Claudia, anyway. I sat by my window and looked at my suitcase. I didn't have much to pack. We were flying back at 10pm. I looked at two bottles that I was given as a gift by one of delegates, they are good bottles, the Italian delegate said. I forgot his name. Aglianico grapes, he said. One them I wish I could have given to Claudia. I like giving gifts. I am sure, I am pretty sure, Claudia didn't turn up either. Anyway, I won't call her. I don't want to be photographed again. In fact, I regret posing now. I don't know why I agreed. I don't even know if I like her or not. But I now know I shouldn't have posed. But it is too late. Too late. I have already posed.

In the evening, I went to the pond on my own. I lay on my back and relaxed while I had a good view of the castle. For a fleeting moment, I saw the man who looked like my uncle standing at the one of the castle's windows. I sat up. The castle had two arched doorways rising from the pond, with the water forming as a ground floor of the castle and another two arched doorways on the opposite side. A further two arched doorways, but smaller in size, on the first floor with a small window on the left. And another wide arched doorway one on the top floor without a roof. I looked at the open doors and open windows.

According to Claudia, the castle was a faithful reproduction of the original. I made a few searches. I found that the castle was built by Emperor Fasilides in 17th century. And now was one of Ethiopia's most sacred sites, and was known as Fasilides bath. King Fasilides commissioned the construction of Fasilides Bath for ritual bathing. The bath was now used for the re-enactment of Timket, the Ethiopian Orthodox Tewahedo celebration of Epiphany on January 19, the 10th day of Terr on the Ethiopian calendar.

The castle. For a long time, I examined everything. The doors and windows, the parapet, the arches and the roofs, the pond and the green banks. It looks like the one I saw it in Gondar. In Gondar. I saw men standing by both sides of the castle facing the pond. There were many of them. Many. The men are dancing in white robes. Men holding colourful umbrellas. Priests wearing colourful robes with sistra and large crosses. Another priest holding a small box over his head. The box is covered in red velvet. Many people beating drums. Men and women with their head covered dancing around the velvet box in circles. I am holding uncle Tesfaey's hand. It is dawn. A priest pleases the water. Young men jump into the pond in their underpants. They are thousands of them swimming. Jumping. Swimming. Jumping.

I stood up and walked to the castle entrance from the back of the pond. Slowly, I entered the Castle. The rooms were airy, dark and empty. I found no one. I looked through one window. The water below, looked serene and calm. I went up to the roof. I looked down. There were few people sitting around the pond. Some were looking at the pond, or at the few ducks and swans floating on the pond. And some were talking to each other, others were on their phones. And some were taking photos of each other with the castle as a backdrop. I walked around on the roof and called my mother.

'... you were with Tesfaye...' mother said.

'Yes, I know that,' I said and sat on to the parapet with my back to the pond.

'You were jumping up and down all day when you came back...'

I thanked mum and hang up. I stretched my body, closed my eyes and breathed deeply. I climbed on the parapet. I opened both arms and jumped while shouting, 'Yeaaaaaaa!'

I landed on the water on my buttocks and my balls. I hit the water so hard. It was very painful. So painful that there were tears on my eyes and I was holding my crotch. I swam quickly towards the bank of the pond. But I realised that the pond was shallow. I stood up and walked to the edge. Ah, it was really painful. I saw crowds of people gathering towards me. I got out of the pond. My clothes were drenched. I was still holding my crotch and walking awkwardly. I then saw a young couple standing in front of me. The woman aimed her camera phone at me. I didn't know if she was photographing my face or my hand which was still holding my crotch.

18

1

My aeroplane made a turbulent landing. I looked at my watch; it was 7:24 AM. The day was Friday 7th June. I stretched my back, arms and legs after trying to sleep curled up for nearly 9 hours, then poked my head out of the aeroplane's door. But instead of seeing the sky and the earth, I found myself walking through a long jet bridge.

At passport control, I claimed asylum. Promptly, I was taken to a screening unit. A female Border Force officer photographed me, then fingerprinted me and wrote me an acknowledgment letter. The officer handed the letter to a male officer who, with another female officer, escorted me in a car to The New Generation Refugees Centre. At the centre, I met other newcomers. I spoke to those who spoke my language but gestured or shouted at those who didn't. At the canteen, all food was new to us and it took many weeks to get used to it. We watched TV in the waiting room, but we fought over the remote control while screaming at each other. In a nearby street, one of us knew how to crack the code on the phone box so we could call for free. We went there every day and called our families.

My room was small, painted in white, though I have seen some rooms painted pink. I wet my bed regularly. I saw a nurse. The nurse said I had a weak bladder. So, I wore nappies. I attended language classes to learn my new tongue.

2

I was housed by the local authorities on the 17th floor of a YMCA hostel. The residents included the unemployed, some ex-offenders, and international students. There were two young boys who'd always sit outside the hostel and look at me with smirking faces whenever I passed them. When I saw them walking on the street below, I spat at them or threw banana peels. Once, while pretending not look at me, they sang together – a familiar song to me, 'We are the world / We are the children / We are the ones who make a brighter day, so let's start giving...'

I went to a grocery store and bought a large watermelon. I went up to my room and waited by my window. And once I saw the two boys walking past, I threw the watermelon. Unfortunately, I missed.

I saw my social worker, Jackie, quite often. Jackie was fat and kind. She helped me with my benefits claims. She filled in all my application forms for me and accompanied me to most of the interviews I was asked to attend. She also took me to supermarkets and clothing stores, to the city centre and fun parks.

I attended language classes 4 days a week. I participated in some activities organised by local charities such as playful learning of English which involved playing table-tennis, table-top football, pool, board games and break dancing.

I was invited by a local journalist to a nearby town to

attend the Annual Refugee Week Media Awards. At the awards, the local journalist, who won the journalist of the year award on an article she wrote about me, titled: *A brief tale of the birth of a refugee*. I had a large picture spread in one of the pages. The journalist gave me a free copy. She told me, through an interpreter, that she wrote the article for me and she hoped that one day I'd be able to read it by myself. The interpreter went through the article with me. The journalist had written exactly what I told her about how my mum was crying at the airport and the part where she wouldn't let go of me. And how my father was holding her back at the airport gates. I also told her that mum was wearing a long floral dress in green and black, with a collar and buttons at the back and belt at the waist and long sleeves. I remember this dress because I chose it for her. Mum had a habit of taking me with her to her tailor so I could help her choose a design from the latest glossy foreign magazines. I only told two lies; my visa was genuine which it wasn't and that I was an only child – in fact I had two brothers and three sisters. After finishing reading the article, the interpreter who was from the same country as I was, turned to me, and said, 'I really, really'—then he lowered his voice—'Don't like you.'

'Why?' I asked.

'I am tired of interpreting for people like you,'

'Why?' I asked while looking at the journalist who was looking at both of us, slightly bemused.

'Do you know for how many people like you I interpret?' The interpreter raised his eyebrows. '10...20, a week. You never stop arriving. I came here 20 years ago and there were a few of us. Now, you multiply like flies. I hate you all.'

'Why?'

'Because people think I am one of you and I look like you

which I am not. No way, you are all idiots. I hate the way you dress. I hate your silly hair styles.'

'But why?'

'I swear to God,' the interpreter said whilst glancing nervously at the journalist, 'If you say, why again, I will lie when I interpret for you.'

3

When I heard the first ever knocks on my door, I held the latch's handle and turned it softly, really softly. They were my friends from The New Generation Refugees Centre. I invited them after the local authorities housed me in a one-bedroom unfurnished council flat. At the hallway, everyone hugged and congratulated me. As I was trying to show them the bathroom, Jamal rushed in and closed the door. I showed them proudly my keys attached to black plastic spiral chain attached to my trousers and took them to the living room, which had a plain blue carpet and four plain white pillows that I had bought thrown on the floor.

'Oh, it's so big,' said Mansoor, walking to the door-sized windows with two small and rectangular windows, one on each side flanked by pink curtains.

'Have you been given money to buy furniture?' Mansoor asked.

'I have some grants from a few charities. Jackie told me that I have enough to buy what I need from a second-hand charity shop,' I said.

'Do you know what you will buy?' Idris asked.

'No, I'm confused,' I said. 'I went to furniture stores and saw furniture for the living room, furniture for the bedroom, furniture for the kitchen, furniture for the bathroom. Furniture for the hallway.'

We entered the bedroom, which had a plain blue carpet and a single mattress covered in a grey bed sheet, a single duvet in a grey cover and one pillow in a grey cover. It also had a built-in wardrobe and a door-sized windows with pink curtains. Jamal came from the bathroom, stood by the window, and said, 'Nice view.'

'Are you going to paint the walls? The colours are worn out,' Mansoor said.

'Yes, I will,' I said, 'But, you know, I want to choose myself. I don't want Jackie to help me. She is insisting in coming with me so I wouldn't go over the budget. I wish I was as rich as Gerges.'

'That rich kid from YMCA?' asked Jamal.

'He used to buy anything he liked, and was so rich that he brought stuff from his hometown to his hostel room; his bed including mattress and pillowcases, a chair, a Persian carpet, drinking glasses and freestanding mirror,' I said.

'If I had your friend Gerges's money, I'd have brought my whole house with me!' Jamal said.

'Your hut, you mean,' Mansoor said.

'I miss home now,' said Idris.

'Gerges told me all the stuff was from his childhood. But, you know,' I said, 'I don't even remember the house I was born into. We left everything behind when we fled. We arrived at that village, near Kassala. Father bought all the furniture and we lived in a big round hut.'

'And what would you have liked to have brought with you?' Mansoor asked.

'I don't know. I shared everything with brothers and sisters apart from my clothes and shoes. So, I am not sure what to think of anything that belonged alone to me.' After a deep thought I continued. 'But I was fond of the chairs. The two chairs. I was with father when he bought them. I chose them. I remember how he was haggling over the price. They were metal frame chairs with yellow and green plastic seats. We, the brothers and sisters, always fought over them when mother and father weren't sitting on them.' I bent my head and pointed at the bottom of my left cheek, 'Can you see? I have still some marks left by my older sister's nails...'

'I guess, you miss the chairs more than your sister now,' said Idris while laughing

'Yes, but I miss the chairs because I lost them.'

'How?' Idris asked

'One day when my parents were away, I was alone playing with the matches and a bed cover. And suddenly, our hut was on fire. I managed to run away. We lost everything. We lived in a shelter for a while. I remember the builders building us a new hut. My father refused any donation of any furniture from our neighbours. He bought us new furniture including four low wooden chairs, but he couldn't afford to replace those chairs. There was no metal paint or plastics available in the shops to paint or repair them. So, the repair man used plain ropes to make the seats. They weren't as comfortable or as beautiful as the plastics. My brothers and sisters hated me because of it, and they hated me even more when I won the drawing lots.'

'What?!'

'I won the drawing lots, conducted by father, to decide who would go abroad between the 3 of us – the brothers only, my sisters were excluded from the draw.'

My friends looked at each other in disbelief.

'At the airport, even though my brothers hugged me goodbye, I felt they'd rather have strangled me,' I said.

My friends laughed uncontrollably, and I joined them.

We entered the kitchen which had its floor covered with lino. The cupboards were bright green. There was a single countertop boiling ring, cheap crockery and a pot on the worktop. I made corned beef sandwiches for all of us and went to the living room.

In the living room, we all sat on the pillows. Idris was still shaking his head, asking, 'But why did he bring them?'

'What?' I said

'Your friend, Gerges. Why did he bring the furniture?'

'Oh! Why?' I said, 'He told me that he doesn't want to forget them nor the furniture to forget him.'

'He thinks his mirror remembers him!' Mansoor said.

I nodded.

'And his Persian carpet.'

I nodded.

Idris shook his head and said, 'Does he believe it flies too?'

'So, you believe what Gerges says?' Mansoor asked.

'I don't know. I am confused' I said.

'So, if you buy second-hand furniture then they will remember their previous owner not you,' Mansoor said, laughing.

'You must buy everything new then…' Jamal said.

'I don't know, but I don't have enough money,' I said

'I am happy that they gave me a fully furnished flat. I don't care about whoever lived there before,' Jamal said.

'I am still on the waiting list,' Mansoor said.

'Me too,' Idris looked at me, 'Why don't you get a job?'

'I am not allowed to work, and I am still going to college.' I said

'Work illegally in the evenings. I do it.' Jamal said.

'£3 an hour? It'd take a long time to save and buy what I want. Besides, I want to send money home,' I said.

4

'Indefinite Leave to Remain!' I shouted when I opened an envelope early on Tuesday morning. The first thing I did was to call Jamal so he that he could help me find a job. Jamal got his Leave to Remain a few months earlier and began working as security guard at one of the city skyscrapers doing night shifts and weekends. He earned decent money. Even though my frame is small, I thought, the work couldn't be as difficult as Jamal seemed to boast. I badly needed to work. My flat was still devoid of much furniture after I went against Jackie's advice and bought – all brand new; a small TV, a washing machine, a gas cooker, a fridge, a freestanding mirror and an extra set of duvet cover and bed sheet with all the money I had from the charity and chose not to buy any second-hand furniture.

While walking to meet Jamal, I saw a young man. I stopped close, behind the man's back. I observed three young men drawing a church in front of him. The man noticed me, glancing me from his corner of his eye, asked, 'What do you want?'

'What are you doing?' I asked.

'Drawing, obviously!' the young man said.

'Why?'

'For my course work!' the young man said, 'I am in my final year of Bachelor of Arts in Interior Design.'

'I am sorry. I don't understand,' I said.

The young man was agitated by my questions, he rolled his eyes, 'You learn to design interiors.'

'What interior?' I said and then I proceeded to ask him more questions, some of which he answered with annoyance and others with pleasure until he closed his eyes and shook his head, and said, 'Man, I am really busy. Please leave me alone and let me do my homework.'

'Can I do it?' I asked.

'Do what?'

'Interior design.'

'Of course! Do you have any creative or artistic interests?'

'Interests?'

'For example,' the young man thought for a moment, 'do you like to draw?'

'I think so.' I said, after a short pause, 'How old are you?'

'21,' the young man said.

'What do I have to have to enter your course?'

'I did A Level in Art...' He then looked at me, and said, 'Well, you can do a foundation course...'

I found the lectures hard to follow; instead, I was daydreaming about my future flat or remembering one thing or another from home, like when I saw a tea pot projected on the screen, I'd remember when I had my first tea with my late grandfather at a cafe; the red tea in a small clear glass when I added six teaspoons of white sugar, whenever I was attending lectures in the History of Design as part of my Foundation Course in Interior Design. At the drawing lessons – the life drawing classes, I got depressed because the teacher said, 'If you can see well, you'd draw well,' and I drew badly; I thought maybe my eyesight was poor. I enjoyed 'drawing objects out of your head' lessons. I drew clouds, wooden boats and moons, suns, trees and rivers. And I liked technical drawing lessons. I drew many pages of one-point perspective of all the rooms of my flat without any furniture in them. I coloured each tile of the perspective in all colours I had of a pack of 24. Other times in pastel shades: yellow, red, blue, green, or sometimes in black and white charcoal. I liked getting my hands and my clothes dirty with charcoal and paint, and I'd never wash those clothes.

I designed my living room instead of a restaurant for our first major project. My tutors didn't seem happy with the primary colours I used. And they also thought it was too obvious and simple and lacked imagination. I was depressed for weeks because I thought I cannot imagine.

Two weeks before Christmas, we were asked to design a Christmas tree on a one-week deadline. 'Design a Christmas tree inspired by your childhood's Christmas tree,' the head tutor, Dermot told us. I knew a little bit about a Christmas tree, but I had no memory of it. I talked to one of the tutors about my lack of knowledge about Christmas trees. In the end, the tutor told me to design whatever I wished. So, I designed my bathroom.

In the second main project, I designed my room. The tutors found it odd that I used Angarêb, my childhood bed. Angarêb was a bed with low wooden frame in palm fibre grid stretching across the bed frame.

In the early spring, my class organised a trip to Florence, but I couldn't go with them because I didn't have a passport.

At the end-of-year presentation, all the students, including the tutors, were looking at each student's work one by one. When it was my turn, Dermot looked at my cardboard scale model, 1:20 the size of my flat at my display. He looked at my designs and then at my drawing portfolio. When looking at my portfolio, Dermot began looking from left to right, but I pointed out to him to look from right to left.

'Oh!' said Dermot.

Dermot put back the portfolio and folded his hands, looked at me, and asked, 'So... tell us about your project.'

'My idea was to design a home for... home for...,' I began.

I was nervous with the tutor's and students' eyes were on me. 'For me.'

Dermot looked again at my model, and said, 'Oh, I see. That is why you have been designing room after room.'

'I wanted to design a place to live in and call it home...' I said.

Dermot looked at my sketch portfolio – I didn't think he paid attention to what I said. He said, 'So you have a photograph of The Crying Boy above your bed...'

'In my village we used have this photograph above our beds,' I interrupted.

'This is kitsch,' said Dermot.

I looked at the students. They were eyeing each other up.

'What is kitsch?' I asked.

'Poor taste,' Dermot said.

'Why?'

'Please, stop asking why..—'

'But I want to know why,' I said

'Please stop asking why,' Dermot pleaded.

'But I want to know why it is like—'

'Why is a childish question, besides, every time I tell you something new, you ask me why,' Dermot took a deep breath, 'The whole year's been why, why... now let's move on.'

Dermot pointed with his index finger at a text on my portfolio – I paraphrased it from a retail catalogue – and read it, softly, 'I created a lounge that I will love with the attention-grabbing Jumbo sofa. A beautiful blend of on-trend textures, the soft jumbo cord and faux leather combine to create a really inviting place to unwind at the end of the day.'

Dermot looked at me and said, 'This is an interior design course, not an interior decoration course.' He put his left hand over his head. 'But why Jumbo sofa?'

'I want to sit on it, cross legged. Sleep on it. Stretch on it. Lay on my back on it. I used it in contrast with Angarêb—'

'What is Angarêb,' asked Dermot.

'Don't you remember? I explained to you a few months ago... It was my childhood bed... You told me its form doesn't work with the colours I was using...'

'Oh, yes, yes I remember,' Dermot said, 'And why are you using those double wrapped yellow and green plastic chairs?'

'But you are asking me why.'

Dermot shook his head.

'We used to have two of those back home...'

'I understand that you are drawing many objects from memory, but you can learn new things here. Those chairs, whatever their names are, are cross-weave strap chairs and are suitable for outdoor use, not indoor.'

I saw most of the students eyeing each other again.

'We used to use them indoors and outdoors,' I said.

'Why not just use contemporary furniture to decorate your flat,' said Dermot.

'I am confused,' I said.

'Why?'

'On the first project, I used contemporary style and you advised me to look at where I came from and pressed me to remember objects from my past. On the second, I designed in the style of where I came from and you advised me to mix the past and the present. Now, I mix them, and you still don't like it.'

Dermot closed his eyes for a while, took a deep breath, then opened them, 'To be a good designer you have to have a good perception. Think of perception. Think of perception devoid of any memory—'

'I don't understand,' I said.

'Your present perception should be acquired as a memory without any interference from your own past. Acquire new memories here; your memories of here and now, and of our past that you will find in the libraries, museums and galleries...' Dermot paused, rubbed his soft black hair then sighed, 'I know where you come from. The fact is simple: You want to be good at interior decoration, right! Then learn its history.'

'Why?'

5

I enrolled onto a Foundation Course in Interior Design History, 1 day a week.

Noel, my classmate, introduced me to Hashish. I smoked with him and on my own, nearly every day. Sometimes, I got stoned at night in the living room while watching TV and fixating on the rooms in my flat. I got depressed by their empty walls, but still, their presence gave me peace. My living room was 13 square metres, my room, 8 square metres and the height of the wall was 2.3 metres. All I had was the basic necessities. My room was empty apart from the bed and few magazines next to it. My living room was room empty apart from the four pillows and TV. My hallway was empty. My kitchen was empty apart from the empty cupboards, the cooker and the pot, the washing machine and the fridge. My bathroom was empty. The only creative thing I did was to change the position of my bed in the bedroom and the pillows in the living room, regularly. And sometimes, if I got paranoid, I'd double check all windows and door were closed shut. My flat was very cold in the winter. The windows weren't sealed well enough and let the cold air in. So, most of the time, I used to sleep or study near the heater. Alas, I could not afford to put the heater on all the time.

In between, I'd revise my notes from our class – mind you, I did my best not to ask the teacher why... People walked on the roofs because they were the streets of the houses made of mud brick and built touching each other with no doors but entered through hatches in the roofs. People slept on the stone beds inside houses made of animal skins and huts made from stone or wattle and daub with thatched roofs... People pissed and shat on clay pots filled with sand while they lived in houses made of mud bricks and layers of walled spaces. The ceilings were painted in vivid blue to represent the night sky, the floors in green, a symbol of the rivers... Houses with mosaic floors, and wall paintings and frescoes... Houses made of timber, stone, and brick. Tables were overlaid with gold, silver, and ivory... Huts where people shared the room with their animals, divided from them by a screen. During the winter, the animals' body heat helped keep the hut warm... Houses that their floors were of hard earth covered in straw for warmth... Houses with large fireplaces... Houses with floors of brick or marble and big beds, raised up on a platform and with carved headboard, footboard, and corner posts supporting canopies and curtains to provide privacy... Houses with stained glass, twisted columns, coloured marble, painted ceilings, and gilt mirrors and oversized chandeliers... Houses with flush toilets... Houses with room walls decorated in gold, bronze, silk, velvet, satin and ornamental door frames and mantelpieces... And... Houses with a clock: Tick...Tock...Tick...Tock... Houses... Houses with central atrium and elevators... Houses... Houses... Houses...

6

While doing another Foundation Course – this time in Furniture Design History – I passed my citizenship test. I attended the citizenship ceremony at one of the city's halls. I wore a black suit, white shirt and a red tie. I borrowed money from The Department for Work and Pensions to buy the clothes. I had to pay the money back in weekly instalments.

At the ceremony, standing, inside a large white walled hall and in a front of the union flag that stood against a blue freestanding screen, I repeated the words of the Superintendent Registrar, to solemnly, sincerely and truly declare and affirm that on becoming a British citizen, I will be faithful and bear true allegiance to Her Majesty Queen, her Heirs and Successors, according to law. And I will give my loyalty to the Kingdom and respect its rights and freedoms. While singing my new national anthem, I looked at the large gold framed picture of the queen, which was placed on a long table covered in a shiny purple/red fabric... I closed my eyes... I walk out of our yard. I close the gate. I am wearing my new dark-red corduroy jeans and dark sunglasses. On the street, I see people carrying a boy and rushing towards me. The boy is my brother. He is crying. He fell from our donkey. His left arm is broken arm and is bleeding from his upper lips. 'How come you dress like this while your brother in such pain,' the people shout.

'Open your eyes,' said the official photographer.

I opened my eyes as wide as possible for I was stoned. I was holding my citizenship certificate with both hands in front of the picture of the queen.

Back to my room and in the night, I dreamt I was back inside my old hut with its circular volume; I covered myself and turned the lantern off and slept. In the morning, I thought for a long about my dream because I once – back home – dreamt to be here, in the very rectangular surroundings in which I was now residing.

Our foundation course teacher was Silberson who was wheelchair bound. In one lesson, he addressed us, 'Today's lesson is about the history of seating. You have to remember that the history of chairs isn't only about form but also about function.' Silberson then ordered us to sit cross legged on the wooden floor and then in a lotus position and then we rested on our lower legs and so on until we all protested. Silberson showed us a black & white drawing. 'It's a library scene at the University of Leiden,' he said. The print was dated 1610. It showed the books, heavy folio volumes, chained on high shelves jutting out from the walls. Students were scattered about the room, reading the books on counters built at shoulder-level below the shelves. They read standing up, one foot rested on a rail, and according to Silberson, to ease the pressure on their bodies. And then Silberson said, 'You complain about me making you sit for a few minutes like that and those people stood the whole day reading.'

In another lesson, Silberson brought in his own Thonet rocking chair. Three of the students, including me, helped him sit on his Thonet. After a brief struggle, Silberson adjusted his posture, and said, 'I really love this Thonet – pronounced toe-net' he caressed its frames, 'Look at its ebonized bentwood frame and natural cane seat and backrest, at its very dramatic and graphic form. See how impressive and stylish it is. It hasn't lost its aura or aged at all. It belonged to my mother. Her mother bought it for her when I was born. It now sits in my house. I am looking forward to the day when I have a child of my own to rock with.'

I put my hand up, and asked, 'Sir, is there another way to love a chair?'

'Yes, of course,' Silberson paused, 'Like falling in love instantly. Have you ever been in love?'

I shook my head.

'How old are you?' Silberson asked.

I didn't answer.

'Never mind,' said Silberson, smiling. 'A few years ago, I heard about a married young man with a child who bought a new brand car, a Mini. A week later, he went with his wife to a furniture store to buy kitchen ware when he saw a modern contemporary reclining chair. He instantly falls in love. I don't know if it was for the shape or material. But I was told this man couldn't stop thinking about that chair and was tormented for days. In the end, he sold the Mini and bought the chair for exactly the same amount of money. £5000. But,' Silberson laughed, 'His wife divorced him.'

In many other lessons, he showed us hundreds of paintings throughout history that contained any type of furniture such as the chaise lounge, chairs, wardrobes, beds, vases and sculptures, ivory and silver, mosaics, oak panelling, plasterwork, stone fireplace surrounds and encaustic floor tiles, carved wooden four poster beds, tapestries hung to walls and velvet fabrics, classical columns, stonework, ironwork and marble, and motifs including swags, garlands and the Greek key pattern, real and imaginary animal figures, decorative ironwork, ornate marble, stained glass and cast iron fireplaces inset with tiles.

One night, I dreamt about one of the paintings. I lay on an ornate four-poster bed made of oak inside a high-ceilinged room. But instead of an angel at the door, my mother appeared.

7

'While the god Melqart was walking on the beach with the nymph Tyros, his dog found a Murex and munched on it. Its jaws were tinged with purple. The nymph admired the colour and asked the god to offer her a cloth with such a beautiful colour. In order to please his sweetheart, Melqart ordered his servants to collect the seashells and to prepare a tincture of this crimson colour, and make a purple tunic that would delight the heart of the nymph...' read our teacher, Jacquie, in the Foundation Course in History of Colour, from her notebook.

Jacquie showed us a postcard picture and told us it was one of her favourite pictures, taken by one of her favourite photographers in 1988. It was a photograph of a pink tulip against a blood-red wall. Perhaps Jacquie thought I was paying attention, for she stood at my table, and said, 'Tell us what you think.'

'About what?' I said.

'This picture,' said Jacquie pointing at the tulip picture.

'I don't know but I don't see anything...' I said.

'Don't you think,' pointing at the tulip, 'Those shades of pink look wonderful.'

I shook my head and said, 'I don't like pink.'

'What colour do you like then,' said Jacquie, visibly irritated. 'We have done the colour wheel,'.

'I don't know,' I shrugged.

'Well, next week's lesson is about subjective timbre.'

'What is that?'

'Your natural mood of thinking and feeling regarding colours,' Jacquie said, looking at me directly.

'My feeling! Ah!' I said, and regretted not having returned Jacquie's gaze.

Just before the end of our course, we visited a gallery with Jacquie. It was an architect's house designed in the early 1880s. After most of the students had dispersed around the rooms, I saw Jacquie standing alone in front of a huge mirror rested above a fireplace, surrounded by yellow walls matched by yellow curtains. Above her head there was a huge chandelier hung from the white ceiling with domed compartments and runs of bead moulding. The light from the windows illuminated her long-sleeved grey shirt and the glittery stripes in her black skirt, ending just above her hips and revealing her long but thick legs. But then I was struck by the similarities between her glittery stripes and the sparkling crystals in the chandelier and the soles of her shoes and the lacquered wood frame of chaise. Furniture, her dress, her body... I thought. But then I told myself, no, no, concentrate... No, I am not doing *fashion* design history course. I opened my eyes and saw Jacquie's head turn around and saw her bangs fall perfectly across her forehead.

'Do you have a boyfriend?' I blurted out.

'No,' said Jacquie. 'But I am not interested.'

I didn't know what to say. In an instant, I went numb.

'So, what is the thing you wanted to show me,' Jacquie said,

'Nah, nothing,' I said.

I hid the postcard sized photograph in my pocket. It was of the Tulip photograph that Jacquie had shown in class the other day. I bought it from the gallery shop, and I wanted to tell Jacquie how much I had grown to feel the photograph.

8

I enrolled on a Foundation Course on The History of Painting.

One night, I was lying on my back on a couple of pillows in the middle of the living room leafing through a book about Hieronymus Bosch paintings. I had had my suspicions but now I found out for certain that I wasn't living alone. I saw a mouse entering and running into the living room. I got up and looked around, but the mouse disappeared from view. Then I saw it running out of the living room. I went to the kitchen and looked around and found lots of mice droppings under the cooker.

The next day, I contacted my housing officer who told me it was my responsibility to ensure pest control. I went to DIY shop. The shop assistant advised me to look for any holes in all the rooms beneath the skirts and then fill it with steel wool and then advised to me to use rat's poison. I located 3 holes in my room, 11 in my bathroom, 9 in the hallway, 23 in the kitchen, 14 in the living room. A few days later, I found a couple of dead mice; one in my living room and the other in my kitchen.

I heard the news that my best friend, Jehar, from my village had died when a snake bit his middle finger while he was digging a hole after a night of heavy rain. He was only 25 years old. I felt guilty because I didn't cry too much. But I remembered how we used to climb Jehar's family tall, white tree covered in dense green leaves, and steal eggs from the birds' nests. I then cried more when I remembered my father's words right at the airport. Father went on his knees – he was over 6 feet tall – and held me by my cheeks and said, 'Boy, come back to visit us as soon as you can. Remember, who is far from the eye is far from the heart.' I dried my tears. I wondered what would have happened if my encounter with the interior design student hadn't taken place and if I had heeded Jackie's advice and bought second-hand furniture. How would my flat have looked now and where would my future be? Perhaps I'd have a well-paid job. Perhaps I could have visited home once or twice. Am I regretting it now? I don't know, I really don't. I looked at my notebook. So far, to design my flat, I had completed foundation courses in Interior Design History, Furniture Design History, History of Colour, and History of Painting. I still have long way to go. I still have to do the foundation courses in History of Reading, History of Photography, History of Flowering, History of Lighting, History of Texture and Fabrics... And perhaps I will add more as I go along... I then went back to study, leafing through a book of Vilhelm Hammershøi's paintings.

9

Because I didn't have that much kitchenware and still lacked a bookshelf, I filled the upper part of the left side of the kitchen cupboard with 45 books. Those books were on the subjects of art history, interior design, furniture and textile design. 31 were books belonging to my old college library that I had failed to return. The remainder belonged to my local library and were so long overdue that I was banned from the library. I also had hundreds of design magazines stored in the lower cupboards. I bought the magazines cheap from a market stall.

And while I was thinking to enrol on the History of Reading course, I frequented a bookshop in my neighbourhood to look at the books and daydream about my future bookcase. A girl with short hair worked in the bookshop. I always felt that the girl's eyes following me whenever I entered the shop. One day as I stood in front of the fiction section, the girl smiled and said, 'Do you know what you are looking for?'

'No,' I said, while looking at the books.

'What do you like?' the girl asked.

'I don't know...'

'Do you like, Realism, Crime, Mystery, Autobiography...'

'Where can I start?'

'Start what?'

'Reading fiction.'

The girl smiled, and said, 'It all depends on what you like—'

'What do you like?' I interrupted.

'Me?' The girl exclaimed.

'Yes.'

'Modern and Postmodern Fiction,' she said, as I looked at her well-trimmed hair.

'Ok, I will start with modern fiction.'

The girl, without looking at me, walked to a shelf and picked one book. It was Alice's Adventures in Wonderland. I bought the book and spent a couple of days reading it. I liked the book so much that I went back to the bookshop to buy some more books, and the girl invited me to her house. In her house, Jacqueline told me that she was moving abroad to do charity work for a few years and that she would be happy to lend me most of her collection, around 150 books, she said.

I was examining some floating black bookshelves at a shop. But I concentrated at one black and thick shelf for a long time. The seller, a middle-aged man, came and held the shelf and said, 'They are stylish. They are sturdy and will hug your wall tight.'

'I'd rather they kiss,' I said, running my hand through the soft shelf's surface.

We both laughed.

However, I could not drill through the wall. I rang my housing officer. The officer told me that all the walls in my flat are of concrete lintels, so I have to use an 'SDS drill'.

After I mounted the shelves and saw all the books on the shelves I felt such joy that could only compare to the time my housing officer handed me the keys to my flat. I then began reading the books.

Shortly before Jacqueline left, she and I had a one-night stand with an unpleasant outcome. I slumped into a depression. Soon, I went to see my doctor. I told her about my problem. My doctor while looking at her computer uncomfortably, said, 'This kind of discussion needs a male doctor.' And referred me to a male doctor. I saw a male doctor. I told him everything about what happened between Jacqueline and me. The doctor was reluctant to talk about the subject; he kept on saying, ah, well, you know...but... However, I was determined on pressing the issue no matter what as I found it so hard to forget about what Jacqueline said to me. Finally, the doctor said, 'Are you sure you measured it correctly?'

'Yes,' I said. 'From my pubic bone to the tip of my glans.'

'Ah, ok... But look, the average size is 5.15 inches and yours is 5.71 inches, so you should be happy. Anyway, you should feel better she said she likes bigger penises not big penises.'

'What do you mean?' I said.

'It means... She didn't say your penis was small...'

'Ah!' I thought for a moment, 'But I've always thought I had a big penis. Whenever I looked at myself naked in front of the mirror, I always thought I had big penis. In fact, I thought mine was too big.'

The doctor looked at me for a moment, and said, 'Can you stand up, please.'

I stood up.

'Take a step back.'

I took a step back.

The doctor looked at me from head to toe, and said, 'You see… You have to think of proportion…'

'Proportion!' said I.

'You aren't that tall, and…' said the doctor.

'Proportion!' I thought, 'Proportion, balance, harmony,' where did I read that, I asked myself. I tried as hard to remember. It must be from a book I read about interior history or an art history book. But, I told myself, I have never heard of history of proportion, and then said, 'So, what is my proportion?'

'Well… You are short. Your upper body is bigger than the lower, and you have shorter legs…'

I slumped on my chair and for a moment I got lost in my thoughts. 'What shall I do with my sleepless nights? I cannot stop thinking about Jacqueline, and now I may never stop thinking about my proportions.'

'I can subscribe you sleeping pills or Prozac.'

'What is Prozac?'

'It is an antidepressant prescription drug. The pill should always make you feel better and happy.'

'But sometimes, I like to cry…'

Back at my flat, I leafed through a book about classical and renaissance arts and stopped on a page about the golden ratio. I took all my clothes off. I stood in front of the mirror. I looked at my body. I cried. I then inspected my reflected face for some time. I discovered that my face didn't have the perfect symmetry. My left cheek was smaller than the right.

'The golden ratio. Fuck. Fuck the golden ratio!' I shouted.

I walked around all the rooms thinking about my height and the rooms' height and width. I then thought of my future chairs and sofas and wondered if they would have the correct fit to my proportions. Sure, I sat on many chairs and sofas in showrooms, but not for long enough to find if they were comfortable, comfortable for my body proportions. I hoped it wouldn't be the same as my jeans or trousers because I have to roll them up all the time.

10

I had an argument with my teacher on Foundation Course in History of Photography. The teacher asked me to stop daydreaming and pay attention to the slides he was showing. They were images from the 1853 Crimean War. I said that I wasn't daydreaming, and then went on, 'There are no battles, explosions, devastations, wounds, blood or tears in the pictures. They are just boring old sepia photographs. It isn't even my historical war.' I then closed my eyes for a bit and calmed down. 'I am sorry. But I am sad today.'

I walked out of the classroom. While walking on the street, I decided to go to a local cemetery. But then I stopped at one of my favourite stores that deals in mid-century furniture. I went in and asked the shop owner, Jameson, if I could sit on the black painted wooden rocking chair. I had chatted with Jameson a few times about furniture and he seemed to have encyclopaedic knowledge. Jameson said, 'Of course, and by all means.' I sat and rocked. I felt a sudden fear engulfing me. My father's words kept ringing in my ears again, 'who is far from the eye is far from the heart.' Though I cried uncontrollably when my mother told me over the phone that my father died, the truth was, I didn't lose much sleep the days the following days. I read and heard about the death of others and I felt nothing. Has my father become another person, after so long not seeing him? I felt my feelings for him weren't that strong anymore. I hardly called my family now days. I had nothing to say. I couldn't tell them about what was happening here, and I wasn't interested in hearing the news about my hometown anymore. Mind you, I had the feeling that all my brothers and sisters would have liked to beat the hell out of me or perhaps even kill me for not bringing them here or even sending money. In the past when I used to call them, I sensed the bitterness and resignation on their voices when I spoke to them. Is it because I had no job, no money or power? Or perhaps they sensed I had no feelings for them apart from a sense of duty that I didn't want to obey. I closed my eyes.

When I felt a hand patting my shoulder softly, I opened my eyes. I must have been asleep. It was Jameson.

'Are you ok?' said Jameson.

'No,' I said

'Oh, I can see. You cried, and then you slept for a couple of hours.'

11

'I don't have a destination.' So answered the photographer Luc.

We walked for hours to the south of the city. And when I wanted to talk to him, Luc said, 'I never talk while I walk.' I got tired. We rested for lunch at a restaurant. Luc paid. Later in the evening, we finished our walk and Luc invited me to a restaurant. At the restaurant, I looked at the menu, but I didn't know what to order. So Luc ordered a starter with a bottle of white wine. The starter was tuna tartare seasoned with capers, basil, Taggiasca olives, onion, extra virgin olive oil and salt. It tasted really, really good with the white wine. Luc ordered the same starter again, then steak tartare with a spicy gorgonzola cheese topping. And when I said how good it was, Luc ordered the same again and another bottle, then the tuna one. Then Luc smiled, and said, 'We need to stop. The bill will be around £130.'

'What!' I said, 'That's twice the amount I get for my weekly allowance when I sign on.'

'I'm paying,' Luc said.

'You know what, once I finish designing my flat, I will cook this and invite you to my flat—'

'How long does it take you? It's been a year since I met you and you are telling me you are still designing your flat ...'

'I am in the middle of...' I paused. 'Learning about freedom...'

'What freedom?' Luc said

'Freedom to choose from historical objects, or rather, from other nations' historical memories...'

'Sorry!'

I shrugged

A few days later, we walked to the west of the city. We rested. We ate lunch. Luc showed me his large tattoos on the left-hand side of his chest, and said, 'Do you have tattoos?'

'No,' I said.

'It won't work on you...' Luc said and burst out laughing. I laughed with him.

'I have seen many black men with tattoos, and they look good on them,' I said. 'I hate tattoos anyway.'

'I like my tattoos,' Luc said.

While we were walking in the east, Luc stopped to photograph a used car supermarket. I asked Luc why he always photographed those kinds of places.

'I look for similarities between the cities around the world,' answered Luc.

'Why not the difference?' I asked

'Err... What!' Luc laughed out loud 'Are you crazy?'

I appreciated walking in silence with Luc. I could think alone while walking with someone. I could see. See everything: houses, windows, doors, trees, plants, flowers, people; their faces, shoes, and clothes. In one long street, I noticed council houses in different styles on one side which looked less elegant compared to the period houses opposite them. I tried to imagine their interior decoration styles. One side, I thought, would be from furniture retail outlets of the kind you find in industrial parks, and the other from some of the high-end interior boutiques that I visit now and then. I also imagined antique furniture as being inherited through generations, just like my teacher Silberson inheriting his Thonet rocking chair, perhaps paired with custom-designed, modern furniture. But, yet again, I asked myself: why do those council houses look more captivating when I see them in exhibitions or photography art books?

In our last walk, we walked for 3 hours to the north east, then a further 4 hours to Luc's flat where Luc had invited me for dinner. Luc's flat had an open plan kitchen/living room. He had a couple of free-standing lamps and another table lamp and another ball-like lamp on the floor. The room looked ambient, dark, and calm. I asked Luc why in almost all interior design magazines the photographs are taken during the day or early evening. Luc replied, 'Because they want to show you the details.'

'But I want to see a mood. Moods. Just like what is in your flat now.'

Luc beamed.

I looked at Luc while he was cooking and told myself this was the last time that I'd be seeing him. He'd return to his home country in a few days.

In the living room, I saw two images of black & white wood engravings. In one of the prints, there was a single piece of white cloth hung on a rope in windy weather. The rope was tied to branch wood stands, uneven in height, on grassland. Behind the grass, there was a river and then a glimpse of a faraway mountain. In the black sky, a half moon. Luc told me that the prints were made by his late grandfather. They were given to him as a gift on his 18th birthday. Ten years ago, he said. I told Luc that this print reminded of something. Luc asked me what it was, but I didn't answer. He pressed me again, but I still didn't want to tell him.

Later on, after finishing our dinner and while we were drinking our third bottle of red wine, the finest I'd ever drank, Luc asked me again of what the picture reminded me of. After some hesitation, I said, 'A long time ago, my mother was hanging our clothes out to dry on a sunny day, early in the afternoon. One of her eyelids quivered and she said that she got the feeling that my father was arriving today. We have a tradition in my country that if your eyelids quivered then you'd get a visit from a loved one you hadn't seen for a long time. For a while, my father worked in a faraway city, and he used to come and visit us once in a while. In those days, we had no means of communication. You wouldn't believe it, but my father turned up in the evening on that very same day.'

When I got back to my flat, I was surprised to find in my bag a rolled paper. I unrolled carefully and saw the same print

I talked to Luc about. Luc must have put it in my bag, I said to myself, or perhaps I stole it, for we both were really drunk. Anyway, I smiled. I framed and hung it on the main wall in the living room.

12

I shaved my afro hair after it began receding at the front. To compensate for my lack of height, I wore platform shoes. I bought a grey newsboy hat and wore it backwards and it fitted with my proportions.

For weeks, I walked around wealthy neighbourhoods to look at the flowers in their window boxes. One day, I was walking along a pavement where the windows of the houses were directly opposite the pavement with no railings. I was suddenly struck by a single terracotta pot. It was rectangular in shape, old and worn with its surface wiped clean with some white crust lines still visible. What a simple beauty, I told myself. I looked at the flowers: they were all red in full bloom. And suddenly I was tempted to steal the box. But as I got closer, I saw that, immediately below the window box on the wall, was a note embossed on to the metal in italics:

"*I reminisced about the days when the villagers' windows were brimming with colourful window boxes until crime forced people to lock their windows.*" Pliny the Elder, a Roman philosopher.

I did an intensive One-Week Foundation Course in Floristry offered free of charge for the jobless. And for a while I looked at the flowers inside the shops from the windows when passing. There was one particular shop that caught my eye.

It's in one of those wealthy neighbourhoods, though the street was unremarkable. Its window was large, split in half by a thin light green metal frame. The interior was designed in a minimalist aesthetic style similar to the high-end designs that I see in high-end design magazines. The window made it easy for me to look at the flowers without the need to go inside. They were placed on one side of the wall and in the middle of the shop. The plants and pots were placed on the concrete floor, opposite. One day I went inside and asked the price of each individual flower. I bought one flower: Midnight Calla Lily. I kept on buying one different type of a flower a week. But one day, the florist, an attractive woman with a long blonde hair but a large black patch at the top – I couldn't figure out if she was blonde or brunette and I could not ask her that because at that time, I was trying hard not to offend people – asked me why I was buying one flower a week. I said, 'One flower, one colour, one feeling a week.' But I doubt if I ever meant one feeling. I wanted more feelings, but I couldn't afford them all at once.

Sometimes, I used to smoke at my balcony in the living room. And while smoking in the summer, I had to endure the horrible sight of my neighbour's garden on the ground floor, below. My neighbour was a nice and friendly woman, probably in her early forties, though my relationship with her didn't go further than polite greetings. From where I was standing, I would say her garden was about two meters wide and six meters long with an ugly pale fence panel. The garden was mainly covered in grey outdoor square tiles with narrow borders covered in soil for the flowers. All the flowers were begonia but for only one large fuchsia. They were in variety of colours: yellow, pink, red, pale red, light pink. The arrangements of the intensity of the bold and bright colours of begonias against the neutral colours of fuchsia coupled with the grey stones arranged around the green leaves made the garden look artificial. Every time I laid my eyes on it, I wanted to shout, 'Kitsch'

One day, I went to the flower shop and asked the florist if there is a way of killing flowers.

'Why do you want to kill flowers?!' The florist asked – she was usually holding flower scissors and wearing a blue worker's jacket, but this time she was wearing a black worker's jacket and her hair was running down across her face. For a moment, I thought she looked like a ghost.

'No! I am not planning to kill any flowers,' I said to her in a calming tone, 'I mean metaphorically... If you want to kill ugly flowers...'

'There are no ugly flowers. All flowers are beautiful.'

'But there are some flowers with ugly colours—'

'No colours are ugly.'

'What the f...' I murmured.

'It is difficult to find them in shops because nobody thinks of killing flowers,' the florist said, 'But you can kill flowers with weed killer...'

On one late rainy night, I filled a toy water gun with weed killer and sprayed my neighbour's garden.

13

I was drunk when I saw a woman in a yellow top on the other side of the dance floor. I stood in front of her. We danced till the music stopped. We kissed till she got her cab. Her name was Natalie.

I met Natalie again outside a tube station. Wow, I told myself: her face is asymmetrical, and yet she is beautiful. Her beauty was calm, not a screamer. As we were walking, I had the feeling that people on the street were looking at us. Perhaps because of my height, I thought. Nat was six feet tall. At the pub, Nat told me that that she was married with two children.

Our third meeting was in a park. We sat side by side. She held me by the neck and kissed my forehead, cheeks then my mouth. She looked at me and then ran her fingers around my face and head and told me how much she loved my bald, smooth head. I slid my head under her dress, between her breasts. I kissed and sucked her nipples while she told me stories about her husband and her children, about her mother and father, about her sisters, her best friend, her friends, her relatives, her neighbours, where she lived all her life, her ex-boyfriends, and her boss.

On our fourth meeting, Nat told me that she felt alone at her family home. From my backpack, I took a book out that once belonged to Jacqueline. It was Samuel Beckett's novella, Company. I lent her the book.

We met at my bed for the fifth time. I hid my tears under the pillow. Why, why? I wanted to scream. I had slept with several women including a few prostitutes in the past and performed well. But why couldn't I do it with someone I love? We lay on the bed naked, holding each other for an hour then for another hour, opposite each other. Then she stood by the window and opened the curtains, and said, 'Why pink?'

'You know I am squatting here. I don't know who chose them,' I said – I painted my room walls in olive green, the bathroom in dark red, the living room in dark grey, the kitchen pure white and the corridor, light grey. I left a couple of paint tins on the hallway floor to give Nat the impression that I was squatting, and that I had just moved in. I looked at

Nat's naked body. She was slim with big breasts. I looked at the tulip photo on the left-hand side of the bed then at Nat's buttocks; they were almost closely aligned in height. I looked away.

On our last meeting, Nat drove me in her black Range Rover around her neighbourhood, just before picking up her children from school. She told me that she was enjoying reading Company and asked me if I'd like to attend a Beethoven concert with her on Saturday. I had never listened to Beethoven before, but I said, yes. In the following days, I spent every day, all day and night, listening to Beethoven. On Saturday, Nat didn't show up. The following week, I had a breakdown.

14

One afternoon, I woke up with a heavy hangover. As I was walking to the kitchen, I saw a yellow light going on and off from my living room while Beethoven's 14th quartet was playing. I hurried in. I saw a street warning light for roadworks, blinking. It was in the middle of the room. I was surprised to see it. I must have picked it up when I was wandering in the streets last night, drunk. I shut the curtains. The room was flashing yellow, ON/OFF/ON/OFF. All of a sudden, I sunk to my knees. I remembered Nat. This yellow light going ON/OFF reminded me of her heartbeat. The yellow. Her yellow top. The music became more and more intense. Suddenly and without any sounds, a camel entered the room through the door, followed by another, and followed by another, and followed by another, and followed by another... Two children run towards camel herds resting on a dry field. Once the children get closer to one camel's back, they creep slowly then they walk on their tiptoes. Then one of the children snatches some of the camel's tail hair, leaving spots of faint blood on the camel's tail. The camels grunt. A man shouts at the children. The children run away, laughing and screaming. The two children make several noose loops from the camel's blonde tail hair. Then they tie them to a flat metal plate with holes. The children plant a small tree branch with several subbranches in the ground. They stick donkey dung on some of the branches and bury the plate underground with only the blonde loops visible. The children spread a handful of white wheat seed on the earth. The children hide away. The magic hour of the sky approaches. A flock of birds descend from the sky. Some birds rest on the branches. A few birds fly down onto the nets. As the birds are eating the seeds, the children run toward the branch screaming. The birds fly away. Some of the birds cannot fly. Their legs are trapped in the net. The children try to get hold of the birds. The birds bite the children's hands with their beaks. There is blood on the children's hands. The children grab the birds by the neck. They cut the birds' heads off. The children walk together on the hills. One of the children holds the silver plate face down, with several of the birds with their heads severed, hanging down. The children put the birds into a pan of boiling water. The children clean the feathers off the skins of the birds. The children cook the birds on firewood. The children eat the birds.

15

I went out clubbing twice a month after I took out a loan from the Department for Work and Pensions. Twice, I ended up in an A & E department. The first time, I got beaten up inside a night club and the second, fell face down on the dance floor, drunk.

One morning after a heavy night out, I was walking home on my own. I didn't know if I was heading east or west in the early morning light. The streets were quiet. I felt calm and my body was chilled. I sat on the stairs of a house door. That night, before I went clubbing, I was at a house party. I took LSD. I was in a white and shiny bathroom. As I was standing peeing, the toilet began to multiply. But I had forgotten to lock the door. Someone came in and saw me peeing all over the floor. I was pushed out and escorted away in front of everyone. I felt ashamed and embarrassed.

Suddenly, I saw the light illuminating the rows of houses in front of me. They were in worn out bricks with false arched windows in rectangular white frames. Ornamental black painted steel balconies decorated with window flowers. Brown chimneys. Ornamental black steel railings and coloured doors. The houses were identical, their windows were identical, the doors were identical. All with an air of total uniformity as if the occupants were denied competing against each other apart from painting their doors in the colours of their choice. I was captivated. I had seen those houses thousands of times before. Perhaps I was inside a house similar to one of those houses the night before until I was thrown out. I had read many books about them. But I had never felt such feeling as this about them. But why now? Why are they looking so beautiful and so present? I asked myself. Perhaps it was to do with the light, I thought. I saw light. I saw the light, I wanted to shout. No, not in that spiritual sense but light itself. This light had escaped me for so long. Perhaps, I didn't pay attention to it. Or perhaps, I had become a night person. Wherever my attention was, I thought, I finally knew how to see those houses or perhaps by now and after all those years, my feelings for them had grown without realising it. It had been a while now since I felt that history had no longer power over me. It was my desire for Nat that had led me to think this way, my desire for Nat alone that let me ignore her past relationships and her husband. And those houses too, which were built hundreds of years ago, and here they were standing: brick on brick, with whatever past memories they have, don't bother me anymore.

16

I joined a job club after the DWP placed me on a 'Back to Work' programme. At the club, they initially showed us how to write our CV which was useful, but afterwards when they began giving us patronising motivational speeches, I told myself that was enough. I found a job as a wall painter for a painting contractor. Among what we painted were the interiors of a few high-rise buildings. We painted the walls, white, room after room, floor after floor, ascending up and up. I worked early in the mornings. I didn't know why, but I tried not to think while walking or working. Perhaps I didn't want to think of myself as a dot among many other dots that I saw, presumably and mostly, cleaners from the third or whatever world, walking away slowly from this or that skyscraper after finishing their early cleaning shifts, vacuuming and sanitizing of all those thousands and thousands of offices.

I also worked as an assistant driver for Jameson in his home removals company on the weekends. Jameson, a middle-aged man with a bald spot, had lost his business dealing in mid-century furniture in the financial crash, and his van was the last thing to survive from that crash. I always remembered Jameson fondly as he once offered me his handkerchief to dry my tears when I cried on his rocking chair that day. And by chance I met Jameson while I was walking and he was driving, and he asked me if I wanted to be his assistant. Through his extensive contacts from his old business, Jameson, established a new removals company.

Working for Jameson opened my eyes to a world that I never knew existed – prestigious auction houses and small furniture business scattered around the city, some dealing in high end, contemporary design and many specialising in mid-century. Though we did small flat and large house removals, sometimes we also transferred single valuable items between our rich clients' properties. One day while we were on the road, I saw a black Range Rover in front of us. I tried to avoid looking at it, but it kept steady in front of us. I shouted at Jameson to stop following the Range Rover.

'I am not following it.' Jameson looked at me. 'It's in front of me.'

'Can you overtake it then, please?' I asked.

'No. I need to be careful with the furniture at the back,' said Jameson then sighed. 'Ok!'

As we were overtaking it, I hid my face with my hand and looked at the driver through my fingers. She wasn't Nat. Jameson glanced at me, and said, 'Are you ok?'

'Yes, I am fine.'

We parked outside what looked like a modernist house. It was almost invisible from the street as it was hidden behind trees. We put the large boxes on the ground floor. This floor had a front-to-back kitchen/dining room with a long, light brown wooden dining table with six light-brown wooden chairs lined up on opposite sides of the table. The sitting room was large with full-height glazed sliding doors leading out onto a long garden. I had been to many beautiful houses with Jameson, to the point where I stopped saying, this is my favourite house. But this house was full of natural light and generous in space. It was like one of my dream houses, but again I had, for some time, stopped daydreaming. The ceiling was in fine polished wood. The floor was in light travertine tiles. On the left, there was a creamy white 3-seater leather sofa facing a low well-crafted wooden coffee table. Behind the sofa, there was a large abstract painting with the colour orange dominant resting against the wall, panelled with hardwood, perhaps yet to be hung. The right side was entirely painted white. The other wall, facing the garden, was covered entirely by shelves yet to be filled with books or exotic objects. A house soon to be filled with life. Jameson and I opened the packages carefully. Among them, there were two identical lounge chairs. The frame was made up of thin red metal bars while a single sheet of light brown leather created the seating. They were beautiful and yet very simple; a cloth and a steel frame that gave them an incredible visual lightness. We placed the chairs against the sliding doors. I asked Jameson if I could sit on one of them.

'You know how much they cost?' Jameson asked

'No, I haven't seen them before. They must be by a living designer,' I said

'£4000... each! Well, go on. Sit.'

'Every time, I am inside this kind of houses, I feel joy and rage,' I burst out. 'Joy that I am surrounded by these beautiful objects. Rage, that I cannot afford them. It's been a while now since I decided to limit myself to study only the last 100 years of home decorating and furniture design. I have immersed myself in their pure forms; emotionally, intellectually, aesthetically. Those masterpieces communicate to me through their shape, curve, colour and material...'

Jameson nodded his head slowly beaming as if he had heard the best words in his life.

'I am thinking to buy replicas,' I said

'No, no, no,' said Jameson.

I saw Jameson's face; it looked as if I'd had committed a terrible sin.

'I cannot afford them. Besides, I am all ok with replicas provided the designer is dead.'

Jameson shook his head repeatedly and slowly.

'Look,' I sighed.

Jameson kept on shaking his head.

'Because of money, I don't mind if those forms are slightly altered and the material—'

'Replicas are cheap because they are bad copies of the original,' said Jameson enthusiastically. 'The materials are bad, and the craftsmanship is terrible. That is why they are cheap to buy. They are another form of kitsch.'

'Ah,' I sighed. After a brief pause, 'But, still...'

'I don't want to hear this anymore,' Jameson interrupted and sighed.

'Ok, never mind,' I said, and closed my eyes. But I wanted to shout: wanker! Jameson might be poor now, but he was rich when he decorated his flat to his taste, I told myself. In design, my tastes are limited by my economic realities, I thought. But I hated the wait. The wait to buy the right furniture for my flat. This wait was unpleasant. But then for the first time, I paid my rent and my bills with my own wages. And my plan had worked the way I hoped it would. I saved enough money to pay for my rent and expenses for the next year. All I had to do then, I concluded, was to work part-time next year to fund the design of my flat and I know when and how.

17

My housing officer, Jack, a man in his early thirties, was at my flat to inspect my newly built kitchen. The work had been done while I was away.

'Please look,' I said. 'Can't you see those cabinet doors and the frames are not aligned with precision? You can see that from the moment you enter the kitchen. Look at the drawers. The spacing between the drawers isn't equal. There is no attention to detail.'

'I will call our contractor. Their team will come and have a look. We have been working with this contractor for a while. Nobody has ever complained about their work before,' Jack said.

'But from the evidence I am showing you, there is a real lack of craftsmanship. Have you heard the saying: The devil is in the detail?'

'All those cabinets are factory made. The workers only assemble them—'

'I went away because I didn't want to interfere with the builders,' I interrupted. 'It has none of rhythm or poise of the yellow and the grey geometric patterns of my old kitchen. Can I paint those new ones?'

'No, you shouldn't touch them. They are the council property,' Jack said.

'You gave me just two options to choose from your catalogue. But this black countertop, those high gloss white cabinets... This kitchen looks totally out of character to the rest of the rooms.'

'This is social housing. We can only provide affordable—'

'I am sorry. I have to disagree. Even if we cut the costs down'—I held my face and shook my head—'It's possible to create elegant interiors and yet cheap. You don't need to have shiny objects in order to hide its poor qualities... Come, come and look at my living room. I designed it with a real desire and heart... It reflects my passions and aesthetics... Please come.'

We both entered the living room

'You see this bookcase,' I stretched both hands pointing proudly at my bookcase, 'It's the main feature in the living room. It's from the iconic Eames house. I copied it and built this smaller version for myself with a carpenter's assistance...'

'It's nice—' Jack said.

'And look... Those four rectangular plywood boxes with their various colours; white, yellow, grey, and birch plywood edges complement well the colour of the solid wood teak mid-century sideboard they are stacked upon.'

'I like the sofa—'

'Her name is Hyda,' I said, 'Her 3-seater embodies the precious feeling of tactile and sensorial pleasure. Though she's ergonomically proper, Hyda inflicts pains on my neck, but it's my own fault. I fall asleep on her with my head on the wrong way while I am watching TV at night.'

'Are you all right?' Jack asked.

'Sorry!'

'You are talking about the sofa as she?'

'Yes, of course,' I said, 'Because every object has its own soul and charm. They arouse feelings in you the way music stirs something. Besides, I say: I fell for Hyda. When I saw her tan premium leather and those narrow-tapered arms and those slim birch legs, in the show room, I felt instantly the same way I felt when I saw Nat for the first time.'

'Who is Nat?' Jack asked.

'A woman with the most well-arranged white teeth and the warmest of lips.'

'Where is she now?'

'Never mind,' I said. I took a deep breath and went on my knees and caressed the oak laminate floor. 'Compare this to that plain old turquoise carpet—'

'You weren't supposed to replace the carpets with wood flooring without telling us,' interrupted Jack. He walked around. As he was about to sit on the sofa, I said, 'Ah! No! No one sits on my Hyda apart from me. But go on, sit on Eames... the rocking chair, please.'

Jack sat on Eames. Eames was a mauve grey rocking chair, covered with a natural sheepskin rug.

'It took me some time just to choose that colour,' I said pointing at Eames 'I took off the pink curtains to bathe the room with natural light. I painted the ceiling in pure white and the walls in soft grey. I wanted neutral tunes. I wanted a lot of light. Maybe it's where I came from, where the sun shines all year long.' I took the yellow cushion off the armchair and sat on the upholstered dark grey Danish wool, facing Jack. 'It's GE 290, by Hans Wegner. It's timeless, isn't it? My father would have loved to have sat on it.'

Jack got up and said, 'I gotta go.'

'Please stay for a while. I have many stories to tell you about each piece...'

'I don't have time...'

'Please, let me show the bedroom. Please come. Just for a second,' I begged Jack, and we both went to the bedroom.

'This is a Compas Direction Desk, by Jean Prouvé. Its elegantly splayed, narrow legs in metal is a formal reminder of a compass. It's an original but a second hand. And this is brand new Robin Day's 675 Chair.' I pointed at the single floating shelf on the top of the desk. 'I designed it and got a carpenter to build it. It was inspired by Lazar Markovich

Lissitzky's Proun room. It looks like a collage, doesn't it? I wanted the desk and the shelf to encompass multiple inspirations that embrace, and this includes the living room, the modernist ethos.'

I stood in front of the shelf, and said, 'I put books that I am currently reading, in this rectangular white box. You know, I had to sand the edges of these Birch Plywood with care, particularly, where the box sits on the long shelf. I wrote *Ways of Feeling* on the blackboard. Well, I don't know why I wrote *Ways of Feeling*. Perhaps out of love or perhaps out of pain. Or perhaps to find the many ways of feeling... but the blackboard is mainly for reminders. I attach my postcards and notes on this grey magnetic board and the chipboard,' I pointed at my built-in wardrobe, 'I am really disappointed with this...'

'This building was meant to be affordable,' Jack said.

'Yes, but it has limited my options. I wanted to buy—'

'I really have to go...'

'Just for a second... One second,' I begged, 'Let me show you the bathroom... Ok... Just the pictures I hung.'

Jack turned his back and hurried to the kitchen. I followed him. Jack picked up his papers and put them in his bag.

'Those flowers were arranged by my local florist,' I said pointing at the vase, 'chrysanthemum, carnation, green spray rose, eucalyptus, copper beech, orlaya grandiflora and blushing bride. I bought the vase, so it can specifically fit to the height of this black retro ceiling light.'

Jack closed his bag. As he was about ready to leave, I said, 'Jack. You are a well-dressed and handsome man. Women love you, don't they?'

Jack smiled.

'Let me tell you one last story,' I said, 'A very little story.'

We both went the living room.

'I bought this African sculpture a few years ago on a Saturday Market. On one stool, I saw this sculpture. She's beautiful, isn't she? And as always, I am strongly guided by my feelings, I picked her up and looked at her intensely. The seller, a Senegalese man, told me that if I have this sculpture in my home for 30 days then a woman would madly fall in love with me. I counted down the days 1,2,3, 4, 5, 6,7...11...14...19...20, 21...29, 30. Nothing happened. Well, a year later, I fell in love with Nat.'

Jack looked at his watch.

'Oh yeah! I forgot the dark brown Persian rug with orange strips. It looks like a Bedouin tent. Doesn't it? And those plants, Kentia Palm, Alocasia, Aspidistra. This is a unique sixties vintage canvas sling lounge chair...'

'You know what, I like the way you decorated your flat but there is one problem,' Jack said

'What is it?'

'How will you move it out of the room?' Jack said, pointing at the bookcase, 'Suppose you were ordered to leave the flat by the council.'

Jack was right. The bookcase was much higher than the door and the window. 'I will always pay my rent and meet my lease agreement, never fight with my neighbours and obey the law,' I said, 'I have imprinted my taste in every rooms' walls and floors. I will fight with all my power to protect my, my... My... Call it what you wish... A flat, an apartment or a house but it's my home. This is the first time that I feel I have a home. And you know what, last month, it was the first time I answered "home" when a friend asked me where I was going to. It's the home I will miss when I am away. Home! I will live here forever. I will never leave my home again... This home inhabits my body and feeling. I feel home and home feels me. I take care of home the same way I take care of my body. If you move me out then you have to move home with me...'

'Well, I... I wish you well. But I have to go,' said Jack and left the room.

I followed him to the corridor, and said, 'Wait. Please let me tell about this original landscape Chinese ink print, those Japanese landscapes, this original photograph. Let me offer you wine. I have a fine wine—'

'Just one glass. One glass,' said Jack, turning back.

'Yes, of course. Have a seat in the living room. What would you like? Château Deyrem Valentin Margaux red or white Broglia Gavi?

'White, please.'

I went to the kitchen and picked out a Broglia Gavi. I looked at the cabinets then at the black countertop. I closed my eyes briefly and shook my head in disappointment. I really hated the black countertop. I walked to the living room. I poured a glass for Jack who was sitting on Eames and one for me then put the bottle on the black coffee table that had two small square mirrors painted with abstract shapes glued on, and said, 'Every night and like a religious ritual, I put on all the lights; accent, task and ambient to create a subtle interplay of lighting in the room. Last month, I nearly jumped for joy when the carpenter who I had dinner with told me that, he felt so settled in the living room that he didn't want to leave...'

'Have you read all those books?' said Jack while looking at the bookcase.

'Yes, I read every single book. 897 in total and counting and that's why I haven't had a proper job for a long, long time. You see, this bookcase has a perfect scale to the room.

The middle part, which is 45 centimetres high, is a display area. I bought some vases and bottles in accordance with the shapes and tonal range of Giorgio Morandi's still life paintings. I tried to be as faithful as possible. I have yet to have time to collect and fill the other two parts with some lovely objects. What objects? I don't know.'

I saw Jack looking at the painting.

'I had to think about what to put on the empty wall above Hyda,' I said standing in front of Hyda. 'I limited my options to Modern and Post-Modernist Art. Initially, I thought to have a reproduction – though I am against all reproduction – of one or two art works with no historical or explicit geographical references or people, preferably abstract, but essentially the art had to be felt. So, in late spring, I went to one of the artists' open studios not far from my neighbourhood. In one tiny studio, I stopped in front of a painting, a large portrait format. On the canvas, I saw diagonal line marks emerge from all sides of the canvas. There were tiny shivers and fragments of colours, brush marks, imperfect rectangular and triangle shapes. The colour pallet selection was in harder hues in thick paint of greens and blues, but the dominant colour was white. But what struck me most, was that it looked unfinished or as if the artist may work on the painting, time and time again. I then thought that designing my flat was just like that - an iterative process. Always, adding or subtracting—'

I saw Jack's face and detected an air of boredom.

'I can put on classical music. Do you like violin?' I said.

'Violin! No way. My ex was a violinist. Nah! I am fine,' said Jack.

'The artist,' I continued, 'was having a drink with some people in the studio and must have seen me looking at the painting with such intensity, for he was standing right behind me. "When do you stop working on a painting," I asked. "Well," he said, "I think there's a moment where you realise that the work demands little or no intervention..." I then didn't pay much attention to what he was saying. Instead, I carried on looking. Gradually, forms began to emerge. On the bottom side of the canvas, two houses emerged. Though I thought they looked like two huts, but that doesn't matter. The houses seemed fractured. They were unrecognisable because their forms were broken apart and seemed to morph into kites. And the kites seemed to get larger as they ascended to the top of the canvas. Almost the whole painting seemed to have exploded into kites... Kites and childhood... I like the visual associations. But I never flew a kite in my life, only balloons. I liked the house on the left-hand side. Then I heard the artist whispering into my ears, "Do you like it?" I nodded. "I normally sell my paintings for £8000 - 4000 each. But because I like the way you look it; I will sell it to you for £400." The artist hung it above GE 290. I told the artist that I wanted to title the painting: *The Feeling House*. The artist told me that I can title it whatever I wanted since it *was Untitled* to him, but then he asked me what I meant by the word *feeling*. I said nothing. I just shrugged my shoulders.'

I saw Jack was about to finish his glass.

'The drawing above Hyda,' I said, 'is by the same artist. It keeps the same spirit of his ideas. It essentially looks unfinished. I commissioned the artist. My brief was simple: Abstract white charcoal drawing on a black paper. What do I like about this picture? The intersections of horizontal and vertical and diagonal lines, though abstract, gives a hint of objects or even landscapes. The pictorial layout, I think, morphs from 2D into 3D towards the right, from exterior to interior or vice versa. When I look at it intensely from time to time, I'd remember stories from *One Thousand and One Nights*. Have you read the book?'

Jack shook his head.

'Never mind, it works so well above Hyda. In fact, they look like a couple; a beauty and a harmony... Sometimes, I even get jealous...,' I said.

'Right, I really have to go now,' said Jack who got up and put the glass on the display shelf.

'Wait, I have not yet told you about my colour scheme for the flat.' I stood in front of Jack. 'Yellow is my favourite colour. I have fragments of different yellow shades everywhere including my mustard duvet cover. I'd like to tell you when I started loving yellow...'

Jack hurriedly moved away from me.

'Do you like the wine?' I said.

'Yes, it tastes great,' Jack said, standing at the living room's door.

'Let me pour another glass.'

'No, no. I have work to do,' Jack shook his head.

'I can cook for you. Cured prawns with peas and potato sauce.'

'I need to go to my next appointment.'

'But I have not told you about that black ink on a paper above the TV. It was a gift from my friend Luc.' I pointed at Luc's grandfather's picture, 'This picture made me rediscover—'

Jack hurried to the exit door. I followed him, and said, 'I have not told you yet about my most precious painting. The painting in my room.'

Jack closed the door behind him, and said, 'Goodbye.'

I went to my room and sat on the bed facing the painting.

I was disappointed that Jack didn't hear the story. This painting means a lot to me. The artist is a friend of a friend. She works on her family past with whatever materials she finds from a generation or two, or perhaps even longer. I gave her a colour photograph of my mother that I brought in with me. In the photograph, my mother, wearing a long traditional white dress, sits on her side, with her face looking towards the camera. I don't know if the artist was inspired by Krapp's Last Tape – she talked about Beckett a few times with me, but she added a tape player and a tape over a dark clothed table. After finishing it, the artist refused to give it to me. But I didn't take no for an answer. I begged and begged and begged. But when I finally got the painting, I wished that I'd have begged Nat the same way to see me again after she had left me. We can see my mother's face has completely disappeared, but we can see her white dress turning, at the end of the photo frame, into a drip of white paint and pouring down over the lush dark blue background and into the tape as if she was a ghost's voice from the past. You know... this picture may help me to remember. Well, I haven't seen my mother for 17 years now. I don't know how or what she looks like now. Well, I have never asked my family to send me any photographs of them and they didn't send any, anyway. Well, I feel... I think my past was erased... No, perhaps I don't mean that. Well, perhaps there are some traces, but they are barely visible from that erasure. All I can say is that my history has always been about erasure and forgetting. I guess I have to pay a price to be here, the way I chose to be... the way I studied the history... A history that folds and unfolds... Or perhaps there was another way, but I chose what I chose... But... I don't know... I don't want to go back.

18

'18!' shouted the interviewer, Jocelyn, a woman in her mid-twenties.

'Yes!' I said, 'It's been a long time.'

'But,' said Jocelyn while looking at my passport, 'Here, it's written you are 36.'

'That is because the home office refused to change it,' I said.

'Because you are 36.'

'No! I am 18.'

'Ok. You are saying, you were born when you arrived here. So, who are your mother and father?' said Jocelyn.

'The state,' I said, 'the state is my father and Eames, my mother.'

'What!' Jocelyn said with a weary smile.

'And like any 18 years old boy, now I am ready to rebel,' I said.

'Can you tell me anything about your culture—?

'I like T.S Eliot,' I interrupted, 'John Soane, Robin Day...'

'Oh!' interrupted Jocelyn, 'What are your roots?'

'Roots! I don't know anything about roots. Perhaps exile has erased them.' I said.

Jocelyn shook her head and rolled her eyes, and said, 'I meant where you came from.'

'I don't remember much anymore,' I said.

'Have you forgotten where you come from?' Jocelyn said.

'Yes, the last 18 years has erased what was before" I said. 'Now, I am only interested in my life here. I have more feeling for my friends here than for the that family I once had—'

'Nobody forgets where he or she come from.' Jocelyn interrupted.

'I did,' I said.

'Where is your childhood home?'

'It is here, in this city. I designed it—'

'Sorry?'

'Yes, I designed my childhood home. It took me 17 years. Do you want to see it?'

'Please let's stop. This job is for someone who is under 20. It's an internship for young people before they go to university...'

'So, you won't take me,' I said.

Jocelyn said, 'No.'

AUTHOR'S NOTES

When I arrived in London, I decided to forget Arabic (i.e. the written form at least; spoken Arabic is different from written Arabic), for then I felt it was the language of a master. I had to replace it from scratch, and perhaps without being conscious of it, with the language of another master. But learning English wasn't that easy, if you take into account my deafness; because of it, my main source of learning was the written word. Perhaps, that is why I studied art and design: even if I failed at it, it was an attempt to communicate in images rather than words.

When I was living in Sudan, I was called a refugee (لاجئ), in Saudi Arabia, a foreigner (أجنبي), and in Britain, I am an immigrant (مهاجر). At the time, I didn't like the terms 'refugee' and 'foreigner' in Arabic, and now 'immigrant' in English. But 'immigrant' in Arabic has a positive connotation. Perhaps that is to do with the prophet Mohammed's migration to Medina and that of his companions to Ethiopia (المهاجرين).

If I had originally written my stories in Arabic, I think I would have over-written them. Arabic is a decorative language. I could needlessly have been lost in sea of adjectives and seduced by its lyrically derived words from (mostly) three root letters.

I am struck by the child-like intensity of feeling I get upon reading an Arabic word aloud now. I couldn't say the same with respect to English, which does not prompt me to utter the word and feel it sensually. However, writing the stories in the limited English I have acquired over these 20-odd years made me write very slowly, as the right words would not come easily. This failure to find the words to express my thoughts and the failure to write a sentence correctly after repeated attempts would often lead me to abandon my writing for long periods. Though time-consuming, this slowness gave me more time to think about what I was writing, until perhaps, my intentions had matured. This delay then would become a creative act. Writing in English, the thoughts lead my writing; were I to write in Arabic, the words would.

I am half Eritrean, half Ethiopian. We escaped the war to Sudan when I was 3 or 4 years old. I barely speak my mother's tongue; Tigrinya. I speak Arabic as well as the Arabs and I speak English well enough (in my own accent) to communicate my ideas. I don't know how I learnt those two languages, Arabic and English, nor do I know how I lost Tigrinya. And this leads me to say that language doesn't belong to people nor is it given; it is found and can be lost too. But I would say you'd be better find it young, and when you find it, let it be erotic.

Saleh Addonia
London, 2022

Acknowledgements

I'd like to thank my friend Vani Bianconi who was there with me when I began my journey as a writer. His support and comments as my first reader helped to shape the stories.

I'd also like to thank those who helped me with edits, comments and supported me throughout, the following: Carla Calimani, Monique Roffey, Glada Lahn, Nausikaa Angelotti, Sajad Kiani, Sara Groisman, Befekadu Yigezu, Anna Leader, Mahmoud Abu Hashhash, Adania Shibli, Rami Bartholdy, Giovani Modera, Xiaolu Guo, Simone Spoladore, Vladislav Shapovalov, Sharmilla Beezmohun, Marta Bakset, Mieke Antheunis.

And my family. My memories forever will be indebted to my grandmother, Mebrat Bashir, my grandfather, Yousif Abdullahi, and mother, Saida Yousif. My brother Sulaiman Addonia and his family; Lies Craeynest, Fineas and Siam, and my sister Amira.

I'd like to thank my publisher Robert Peett for believing in me and my stories, and his team including Poppy Britcher.

And for enabling me to continue writing: The Royal Society of Literature and The Arts Council.

Helen E. Mundler

Three Days by the Sea

No-one talks about Susie but no-one can forget her – until Gina and Robert receive invitations to a family reunion by the sea in Cornwall.

As the three days unfold, the stories and secrets of each character are mapped against England's changing society through the history of the family. Gradually, the truth of Susie's disappearance over twenty years ago is revealed as the secrets, griefs, and eccentricities of one family are exposed to the Cornish light.

Three Days by the Sea is a subtle, funny and moving story of hope and renewal. With dry, sharp humour and warmth, Helen Mundler unpicks the trials and tensions of family life.

Publication: 19th May 2022
(Hardcover) ISBN: 978-1-910688-69-4

Ashutosh Bhardwaj

The Death Script:

Dreams and Delusions in Naxal Country

A haunting ode to those who paid the ultimate price—through the prism of the Maoist insurgency, Ashutosh Bhardwaj meditates on larger questions of violence and betrayal, love and obsession, and what it means to live with and write about death.

From 2011 to 2015, Ashutosh lived in the Red Corridor in India wherein the Ultra-Left Naxalites, taking inspiration from the Russian revolution and Mao's tactics, work to overthrow the Indian government by the barrel of the gun. He made several trips thereafter reporting on the insurgents, on police and governmental atrocities, and on the lives caught in the crossfire. *The Death Script* chronicles his experiences and bears witness to the lives and deaths of the unforgettable men and women he meets from both sides of the struggle, bringing home the human cost of conflict with astonishing power. Narrated in multiple voices, the book is a creative biography of the region, Dandakaranya, that combines the rigour of journalism, the intimacy of a diary, the musings of a travelogue, and the craft of a novel.

The Death Script is one of the most significant works of non-fiction to be published in recent times, bringing often overlooked perspectives and events to light with empathy. Praised by India's topmost scholars and critics, the book has already won various awards.

Ashutosh Bhardwaj is a bilingual fiction writer, literary critic, and is the only journalist in India to have won the prestigious Ramnath Goenka Award for Excellence in Journalism for four consecutive years. As a journalist, he has traveled across Central India and documented the conditions of tribes caught in the conflict between the Maoist insurgents and the police.

Publication: **4th August 2022**
(Hardcover) ISBN: 978-1-910688-86-1

Cass J McMain

Rescuing Barbara

'Subdues one into complete and horrified fascination ... The effects of a work like this linger for days' *Karen Jennings* (*An Island*)

Ignoring her mother may have been a mistake.

During a bout of sobriety, Barbara implored her young daughter to turn her back on her if she began drinking again. Exhausted by her mother's alcoholism, Cass McMain finally took this advice and ignored everything the woman said or did for many years. She did not return calls, she did not visit, she did not react, send letters, or cajole. She simply turned away and waited for her mother to hit bottom or die trying. But as she discovered, bottom may be much farther down than one expects. Eventually, she is forced to wade in and untangle the mess her mother has created.

A gripping series of moments –painful, loving, desperate – *Rescuing Barbara* is a bitterly funny, and even lyrical true story about the inherent dangers of detachment ... and a reminder that predators are everywhere, waiting to fill in the gaps.

Publication: **2nd June 2022**

(Paperback) ISBN: 978-1-910688-40-3

Anees Salim

The Bellboy

Latif's life changes when he is appointed bellboy at the Paradise Lodge –a hotel where people come to die.

After his father's death, drowned in the waters surrounding their small Island, it is 17 year-old Latif's turn to become the man of the house and provide for his ailing mother and sisters. Despite discovering a dead body on his first day of duty, Latif finds entertainment spying on guests and regaling the hotel's janitor, Stella, with made-up stories. However, when Latif finds the corpse of a small-time actor in Room 555 and becomes a mute-witness to a crime that happens there, the course of Latif's life is irretrievably altered.

'There's no other way to put it: Anees Salim [...] is one of the most affecting writers working today. As prodigiously talented as he is, he is distinguished from his contemporaries writing in English by his precision in identifying and then mining the deep fatalism that runs through the Indian psyche.'
Mint Lounge

Publication: **July 14th 2022**
(Hardcover) ISBN: 978-1-910688-67-0

Anees Salim's books include Vanity Bagh (winner of The Hindu Literary Prize for Best Fiction 2013), The Blind Lady's Descendants (winner of the Raymond Crossword Book

Award for Best Fiction 2014 and the Kendra Sahitya Akademi Award 2018), The Small-town Sea (winner of the Atta Galatta-Banaglore Literature Festival Book Prize for Best Fiction 2017), and The Odd Book of Baby Names. His work has been translated into French, German and several Indian languages